QUARKS

OF

NATURE

A Magical Journey Through Time and Space

BRAD UHRICH

To Rhonda, my real-life Linda,
my soulmate, my confidante and
my best friend.

To John, Dana, Jenai, and Leah
I say Dream Big.
If I can write a novel at my age,
imagine what you can do at yours.

To the memory of
Robbie Joe, Michael, and Robin
who were stolen from us well before
their time.

Table of Contents

Table of Contents

Table of Contents

My apologies to all the real scientists and physicists in the world without whom we would not understand how our world works and what holds our universe together.

Without you, I would not have been able to generate such large volumes of technobabble with intentions no more noble than casual entertainment.

Who knows, perhaps this book will pique the readers' interest in science enough to be motivated to determine for themselves where in this story the science fact evolves into science fiction.

"Sean, it's not working."

"Not working? What's not working?"

"The fermion phase inverter. It's not working. The rate of assimilation is 1.6 times the rate of inversion."

"Can you be more specific please? If it is not working there can be no rate of inversion. So, is it working – yes or no?"

"Sorry. Yes and no. The fermion phase inverter is functioning, in fact, I'm pushing it at an oscillation rate 22 percent above the sustainable threshold. It is doing exactly what it is supposed to do. But that is just not enough, it's not even keeping up. This is not the answer. And we're running out of time."

"How much time do we have?"

"Just a sec... The rate of assimilation is no longer linear; it has gone hyperbolic. Switzerland and most of Austria will be gone in less than six hours. At the current rate of acceleration, no one on this planet will see tomorrow."

"Well shit! We're out of time and out of options. We're going to have to try it, aren't we?

Cheng Le obliged me with a simple sad confirming nod.

1. THE BEGINNING OF THE END

> *Whatever can happen, must happen*

HOW IT ALL ENDS

I'm Sean Blake and my day is off to a very horrible start, which is a rather arrogant self-pitying statement given the much worse day others in the world are having because of me. The year is 2066, make note of that because it will be important later (if there is a later). I would continue the story I started but it will end shortly and you will have no better understanding of what is going on or how I caused the imminent total annihilation of all life on this planet. No, I'm going to have to start at the beginning and relate the relevant events in sequence of occurrence in order for you to make any sense of this.

You should understand right up front that I can only tell you the first part of the story. The next part (and I hope there is a next part but I can't be certain of that) will have to be relayed to you by someone else. That's because when I push a certain button in about ten minutes my existence as I have always known it will cease. No, I'm not committing suicide per se, but the effect will be nearly the same. You see, I'm about to attempt to send a message to my former self six years ago. There is a near certain probability that this will alter my/our past and your, our, and his (Sean of six years ago) future. At least that is the hope and the plan. It is impossible to know exactly what will happen, but before you label me reckless you must consider the risk vs. reward factor. The potential risk is admittedly through the roof, metaphorically speaking, but then again, the potential reward of any possible future other than total annihilation is, again metaphorically speaking, stratospheric.

I'm just hoping that I was smart enough six years ago to listen to me when I tell me what to do.

But I'm confusing you. Let's start at the beginning.

How it Begins

I wasn't always a highly respected and esteemed pinnacle of quantum physics knowledge. By normal standards, largely due to my gift for math, I had a short childhood. That's not to say I didn't get into trouble like almost every kid does. There were things I did with my neighbor Robbie when I was nine that I'm not proud of and I have never told anyone.

Math has always come easy to me, easier than even English (I remember learning the hard way in a sixth-grade spelling bee that "physics" doesn't have an "f" in it). Algebra, trigonometry, factoring, all those things just seemed to be baked into my brain from birth along with an innate and intense desire to learn everything – well, everything I was interested in. Because of that, my parents and teachers always put me in accelerated classes and I skipped a number of levels, first in grade school then completing high school in just 2 years, all the while completing some college level introductory math classes simultaneously. Like I said, math was as easy for me as watching Star Trek.

All of this advancement was OK with me, I still had a life outside of school, but I was bored. Nothing really excited me and most of my daydreams were spent wondering how the starship Enterprise could travel back in time to save the whales (and all of humanity) by speeding toward the sun then at just the right moment break away from the sun's gravity and slingshot back into the twentieth century. I know it was fiction just for entertainment but I couldn't help wondering, '*You know, there might be something to that.*' But that's where it ended, just wondering.

That was until I went to college and Dr. Yashiki Kimura entered my life. He was a phenomenal teacher who provided me all I needed to discover my life's passions. I don't know how he was able to look beyond that punk image I proudly portrayed of myself and open me up to a fantastic world that few people know about but is literally right at our fingertips – and yes, I use the term "literally" properly (at least I'm pretty sure).

The Music Trail

At the time, I fancied myself a musician. I loved how it was possible to weave sonic patterns of vibrating gases in such a way as to elicit hugely powerful emotions from listeners. Guitar was my instrument of choice and as with every beginning guitar player I learned early on that if you don't press firmly on a string in exactly the right place, the sonic result will be more of a buzz than a tone. I spent months training my fingers to play three chords with which I was then able to play a seemingly unlimited number of songs. *Long live Rock and Roll!* After my skills became more advanced it was ironic to learn that there are certain locations on the fret board where not only is heavy pressure not required but in fact must be avoided to elicit beautifully hollow harmonic tones. It was counter intuitive that the prettiest sounds resulted from the lightest touches.

I thought I was being musical when I discovered the intriguing nature of these harmonics but I think in hindsight, I was really just fascinated with the math behind it.

To produce a harmonic exactly one octave higher than the open string, you touch ever so lightly at the twelfth fret. Not coincidently there happens to be 12 notes in a diatonic scale. Also curious is that if you measure with a tape measure you find that the 12th fret is positioned exactly halfway between the nut and the bridge (guitar terms for the two ends of the strings – nut is close to tuners, bridge is on the body).

Experimentation quickly shows by touching at the 12th fret (1/2 of the string length from nut to fret) and picking the string, the vibrations split the string exactly in half and have 2 distinct vibrations at the higher pitch in both halves of the string. The same holds true for touching at the 7th fret (1/3 of the string length) and the 5th fret (1/4 of the string length). These cause three vibrations of 1/3 length producing a tone a perfect 5th higher and four vibrations of 1/4 length producing a tone two octaves higher respectively.

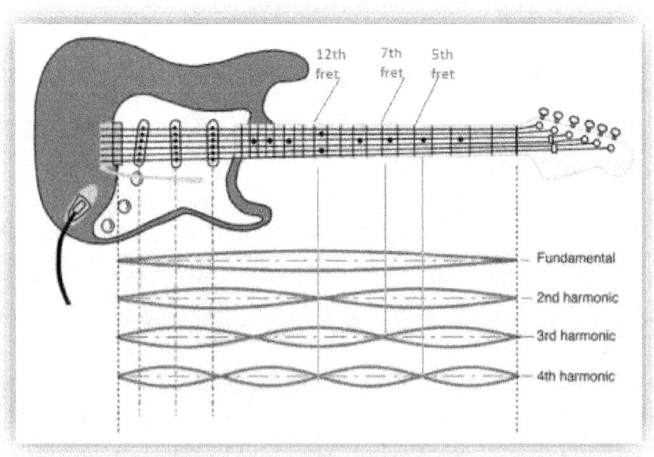

The waves produced by these vibrations are directly analogous to waves found in the forms of energy which Dr. Kimura will eventually lead me to understand. But that is not going to happen yet for a few years.

The natural evolution of my love of music and math progressed into the world of computer science. Artificial Intelligence (AI) had become a real "thing". Anything and everything back then was becoming the product of AI in some form or other − at least that's what the corporate world was selling to people. I was constantly befuddled as to how a computer could be considered more qualified to formulate the proper blend of wool and nylon to use in my thermal socks than a person who once went camping with only cotton and polyester blend socks. In my view, those life lessons can be infinitely (and I do not use "infinitely" literally) more valuable.

I watched as AI consumed everything, even the arts. Given the mathematical patterns in music coupled with the vast amount of sample data available, it was inevitable that some misguided but well-intentioned scientists would utilize AI for 'writing' music. The thought was that they could 'bring out the inner artist' in everyone. With all the technological advances being made, natural instruments − strings, woodwinds, brass − were being replaced with advanced synthesizers that were capable of tweaking every aspect of the soundscape, even down to the most subtle articulations. Great effort went into preserving, or rather simulating, such things as the breath noises made by a flautist and the natural out-of-tune characteristics of most brass instruments that give them that "fat" sound. Human interfaces were developed to allow any person to customize their play list – not in the old-fashioned way of selecting from a list of recorded songs from their favorite artists but rather customizing the characteristics of the computer-generated music to match their mood. One could increase the tempo, swap the instruments, add more ambient tones, transpose to different keys, pretty much anything to fit the current mood of the listener. If you loved a particular tune but found the male vocals grating, just replace them with vocals of a soft, sweet female voice. Is the guitar distortion a bit too much? Swap it out for an acoustic guitar or just for fun, make it an oboe.

The problem that occurred, as has been seen in many fields of science, is that the technology advanced at a speed far greater than the speed at which man was advancing in his capability to use it. The possibilities became so vast and intertwined that very few fully understood everything. Normal people got frustrated spending inordinate amounts of time customizing songs, so a new market emerged where people could just purchase finished sound productions (can't use the term 'recordings' because rarely during the production was there ever an audible sound to record – it was all just digitally generated data that was stored without having never been heard). The industry had gone full circle.

People were now selecting music from libraries of generated music by their favorite engineers. The big difference being this new 'music' was missing the heart, soul, and inspiration of an artist. The engineers were just putting digital lipstick on a computerized pig.

I wanted nothing to do with it.

LOVELY LINDA

The most truly beautiful thing about music is not what I did for it but rather what it did for me. Music was instrumental (pun intended) in introducing me to Linda Ostranger, my soulmate.

I met Linda at a dive bar on campus called the *Come on Inn* one weekend when I was the entertainment (the double entendre in the name was so appropriate for a college campus). The bar didn't pay me anything and they wouldn't let me charge a cover to get in, but they did allow me to put a hat on the tiny stage and accept tips. In my mind that was a perfect arrangement because I would have never paid to listen to me. I'm pretty certain the tips I got were simply pity tips from benevolent souls wanting to help out a struggling college student who was just trying to get by. That worked for me too. Some nights I raked in over twenty bucks. I do however, still to this day remain skeptical about that one Saturday night when the bar crowd appeared to thin out when I started my set and remained thin until a fuse mysteriously blew for the outlet on the stage. While management was looking for a spare fuse the bar filled and a fuse was suspiciously never found.

Linda (I learned her name from the bartender) was a now and again patron on weekends though she never stayed long when she came. She always sat near the stage but never next to it. When she came with a friend, I noticed that her friend was the one with her back to me and I could always see Linda's face. I figured that meant something but didn't know what. At a time when my social skills were every bit as clumsy as my song writing skills, I had developed inexplicable and immensely strong feelings from afar for her and possessed absolutely no social tools or savvy about how to express them. For one thankfully brief and fleeting moment I entertained the idea of using my formidable math skills to introduce myself to her by formulating an algebraic equation depicting the logarithmic curve representing the summation of the ratio of her mutual acceptance (m) times my affection (a) times the speed of light (c) squared over my love (L) as time (t) progressed from now (n) to infinity (∞).

$$f(\alpha) = \sum_{n=1}^{\infty} \left(\frac{m\alpha c^2}{L} \right)$$

As time approaches infinity (∞), the linear expression of her acceptance over my love would converge on a universal constant. That should surely win her over.

It was only when I found myself considering a "lemon meringue π" reference that reality smacked me on the side of the head and better judgement won out. I canned that idea.

That forced me to fall back onto my questionable talents as a singer-songwriter to come up with something artistic, expressive, and whimsical that would profess my irrepressible love for her and win her heart. One night when she was there alone, I sucked up the courage to sing the song as my final song of my first set. I can't recall exactly what it was but it was titled *Linda, oh Linda* and it went something like this:

Linda Oh Linda
I'm out of my mind
Linda Oh Linda
You're one of a kind

Linda Oh Linda
You're really fine
Linda Oh Linda
I'm going to make you mine

Once concluded I stepped over to her table and introduced myself then asked if the seat next to her was taken. She invited me to sit so I asked her her name. She told me and I feigned surprise while replying "What a coincidence! That's the name of that last song." To her credit I will be forever indebted to her for suppressing her laughter until after I was out of earshot. It demonstrated amazing strength of character and control on her part. Instead, she leaned over with the kindest of smiles and kissed me on the cheek saying simply "I am <cough> blessed." Some might say that wasn't an inadvertent <cough> but rather an involuntary blurt of amusement and to reinforce their argument they might postulate her sweet smile was nothing more than a mischievous combination of grin and smirk. I, however, know how to recognize a kind smile and simple clearing of the throat. Besides, all that speculation is moot anyway because I knew from that moment forward unto the end of time as we know it, she would be my soulmate and I hers. All that was left was for us to get to know each other.

Dr. Yashiki Kimura

Immediately upon enrolling in college I had the good fortune to get Dr. Yashiki Kimura as my professor for *Newtonian Physics 201*. I was able to skip a number of 100 level classes because of my penchant for math. I had no particular interest in Sir Isaac Newton beyond historical recognition that he created calculus. The class did, however, meet the requirements for three credits of core curriculum and I also recognized that his work was backed by lots of formulas and algorithms so I figured I would breeze through it with little effort while I tried to find my passion.

Dr. Kimura, or Yoda-san as his students had affectionately and appropriately nicknamed him, was a friendly man of indeterminate age – maybe forty-three years old, maybe seventy-three, I couldn't tell. He had short thinning hair and wore John Lennon glasses. After one week of instruction, I was struck by his passion for teaching and his ability to explain highly complex concepts in a way that a twelve-year-old could understand. He was a warm hearted and brilliant man who exuded confidence and compassion. In informal situations he appeared flattered to be referred to as Yoda-san.

On one particular day that I will never forget he got a tad bit tangential while explaining one of Newton's three laws of motion. Somehow, he got off onto wave particles and their associated properties of phase, amplitude, and direction and what happens when waves collide. Now he was fully capable of throwing out big terms like *Constructive Interference* and the *Superposition Principle* and even throwing in formulas and graphs for the amplitude of waves like this:

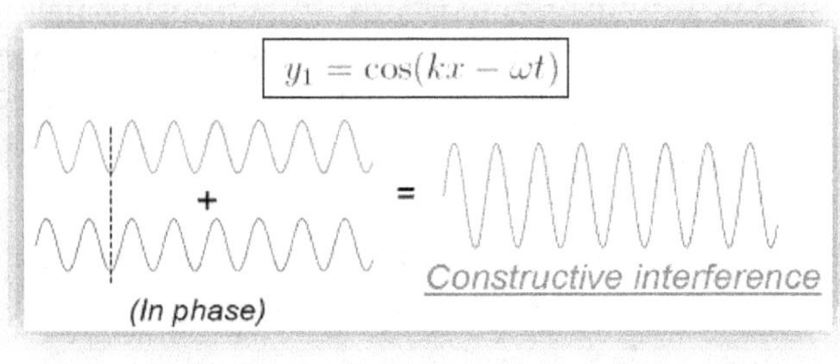

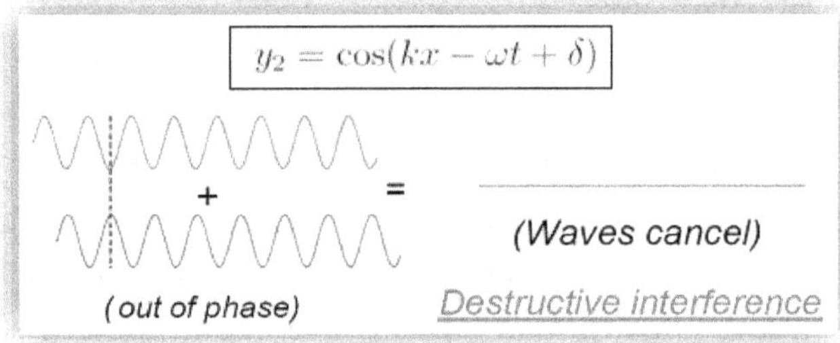

And he did so, but he didn't stop there. Instead, in a matter of minutes, he described quite succinctly and visually each one of those properties by the use of a fifteen second video clip of two rocks dropping in a smooth pool of water. He explained how wave energy is additive and how two waves of the same amplitude and phase will combine to make a new wave twice the amplitude while waves of opposite phase will cancel. But it was the visual he used of water in a pond that made it all make sense. He had an amazing ability to relate the abstract in very physical and observable way.

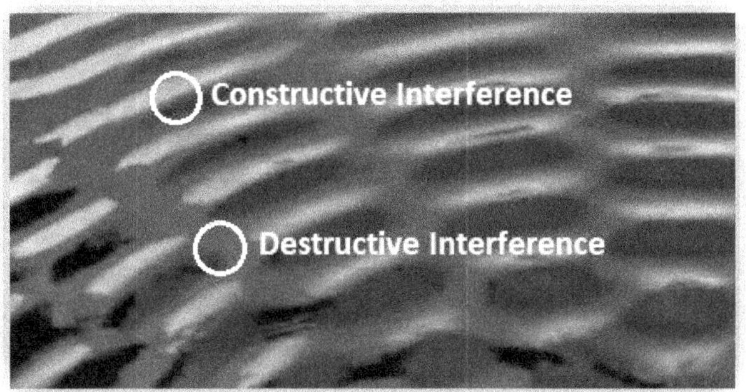

Granted, this was not the most complicated concept in the world but it is more about the method than content. If that was how he taught all of his classes I was going to sign up for every class he taught – even if it was Home Ec.

QUANTUM MECHANICS

After looking at the curriculum catalog and finding a class called *Intro to Quantum Mechanics* which he taught, I immediately approached him to see if he would allow late enrollment. He asked me how comfortable I was with the large amounts of advanced math involved. Without thinking, I immediately responded by telling him my lemon meringue π joke. I promptly wished I could have that one back. He amicably shook his head and with closed eyes dipped his head, but I distinctly saw the hint of a suppressed smile on his lips. He then said quite pseudo-formally "It will take much more than that, but it's OK with me."

I was in!

That class changed my life. I became entrenched in learning everything I could about bosons, photons, fermions, leptons, hadrons, muons, and Klingons[1].

The best advice that Yoda-san ever gave me for understanding the science at a quantum scale was to become like a two-year-old child. Divorce yourself of all the preconceived notions you have developed over a lifetime of working and interacting with objects in the large-scale realm. He instructed that as long as you persist trying to make quantum behavior align with classical behavioral concepts you will always be saying to yourself "I don't understand" or "That makes no sense". Applied in that way, both statements will be true but neither will be helpful in any way.

Right out of the gate I ignored this advice as I tried to rationalize how it could be possible that the laws of physics that we have developed over centuries, laws that were good enough to put a man on the moon, were

---

[1] OK, Klingons really have no place whatsoever in the quantum world but I liked learning about them nonetheless. Photons do have a place, just not in the way depicted by the torpedoes Captain Kirk would occasionally fire on deserving adversaries.

somehow not adequate for explaining behavior on the small scale. That thought process was quickly altered by Yoda-san's absurd but effective analogy.

"Imagine," he began, "you're sitting at home and your dog comes over to elicit some affection. You scratch his ear, pat his head and he's content. You look down to see a flea has landed on the coffee table and you inexplicably feel compelled to show the exact same affection to her. However, when you pat the flea's head in the same way there are disastrous consequences for the flea. Now I ask you, did the same rules apply at the small scale or not?"

The answer to this, as well as a nearly every other question in quantum physics, is as it turns out, both yes and no. Once I could get my head around this my rate of comprehension increased exponentially.

I learned the quantum realm is comprised of waves, particles, mass, and energy that peacefully and cooperatively exist in a constant state of controlled chaos. Things simply can't be observed in the way we observe everything else. It is probably this radical nature that I found so appealing. At the core of this are concepts like the *Observer Effect* [2] and the *Heisenberg*

---

[2] In physics, the *Observer Effect* is the disturbance of an observed system by the act of observation.

Uncertainty Principle[3] that define and explain what can and cannot be accurately observed.

I never had a problem with the *Observer Effect*. I am of the opinion that every single person in the modern world can attest to that effect by virtue of their own experimentation. I'm referring to the experiment we have all done, whether we admit it or not, where you attempt to verify that the light in the refrigerator really goes on and off when you open and close the door. By opening the door, you alter the result of the observation.

The *Heisenberg Uncertainty Principle*, on the other hand, was harder to comprehend (and impossible as long as I continued to apply large scale thinking). On the surface it seemed implausible to me that measuring both velocity and position simultaneously was impossible. I had watched modern day drag races before and those measurements happen with perfect accuracy for every race I argued. A laser triggered camera is placed on the finish line and when triggered it simultaneously instructs a camera to record the position and a computer to compute the car's speed. Perfect simultaneous and accurate results, right?

---

[3] The *Heisenberg Uncertainty Principle* states that due to the wave-particle duality of matter, it is impossible to measure or calculate exactly, both the position and the momentum of an object.

Yoda-san's response… Yes and No. I would in time get used to this ambiguous answer.

He then took me through the following analysis. "When the race car interrupted the laser beam's stream of light it still took time for that part of the beam that was already enroute to get to the other side. Just like when you shoot a stream of water from your lawn hose then quickly kink off the water supply. The hose stops immediately but the arch of water already in the air still takes some amount of time to complete its arch and land on the ground. Then, once the gap in light arrives and triggers the computer, a series of computer steps occur but each of those take time also[4]. A few nanoseconds here, a few there and pretty soon you have some number of microseconds. Once you add the time taken for the camera and computation those microseconds can turn into a full millisecond. Now if all you need to know is whether the Ford beat the Chevy then that level of accuracy far exceeds your needs and the error is deemed immeasurable. If, however, you're trying to measure how far an electron traveled in that same millisecond the measurement is completely worthless." He then concluded, "I'll save you the math work, an electron would travel 186 miles in a single millisecond."

---

[4] Flipping a single bit in a computer register takes approximately 10^{-9} seconds. Flipping a qubit in a quantum computer is much faster at an estimated $2 * 10^{-16}$ seconds but let's not get ahead of ourselves.

As I started to incorporate these and other principles into my thought process I began to understand, without translation, the quantum world. I found it analogous to when I studied German in high school. There came a time when I actually started to think in German instead of rapidly translating English thought into verbal German. Understanding that bouncing a photon off of a lepton in order to 'see' it necessarily alters that lepton's properties became second nature and very natural way of seeing things.

One topic that occasionally but persistently surfaced was that of Einstein's theory of *Special Relativity*. I felt reasonably confident with my knowledge of *General Relativity* but was picking up insinuations that perhaps quantum mechanics was challenging some of Einstein's most important and most highly scrutinized work. Einstein was known to describe certain aspects of quantum mechanics, most notably *quantum entanglement*, as "spooky action at a distance". That intrigued me. I just had to gain a better understanding.

Time Dilates

Albert Einstein became one of my all-time favorite characters. Not only brilliant and insightful but with a sense of humor to boot. He is the one who taught that when observations don't seem to match common sense then maybe it is common sense that is the problem. He had a beautiful way of viewing life. There were gaps in Isaac Newton's definition of gravity that Einstein was intent on explaining, essentially trying to reconcile Newton's laws of motion with new emerging laws of thermodynamics. In 1905, he published the result of that work as his theory of *Special Relativity* and then later with his theory of *General Relativity*.

I became enamored with the concept of our four-dimensional existence, specifically the three dimensions length, width, and depth along with the fourth dimension of spacetime. Space can no longer be thought of as a fixed emptiness. Space is a thing that can bend and warp. Likewise, time is not linear or just something that passes and nothing can be done to change the rate at which that happens. Time does in fact dilate and stretch. Special relativity teaches that those objects travelling at high velocity experience time passing more slowly. The closer an object's speed gets to the speed of light, the slower time passes (for that object). Conversely, I learned that objects impacted by less gravity experience time passing more quickly.

One of the first experiments to demonstrate this was performed in 1971 by Joseph C. Hafele, a physicist, and Richard E. Keating, an astronomer. They took four cesium-beam atomic clocks (the most accurate clock in existence at the time) aboard commercial airliners (pictured on the right). They flew twice around the world, first

eastward in the direction of the Earth's rotation, then westward against the Earth's rotation, and compared the clocks against others that had remained on the ground. The results matched their predictions with near perfect accuracy. The Eastbound plane lost 59 nanoseconds and the Westbound plane gained 273 nanoseconds with a combined margin of error of less than 20 nanoseconds.

Think of the implications of that!

The pilot of the Westbound plane who kissed his wife goodbye before leaving, returned and kissed her hello 273 *nanoseconds into her future!* She missed out on sharing 273 nanoseconds of her married life with him.

'Isn't that time travel?' I postulated to myself. I couldn't find an argument to the contrary.

Further study enlightened me to countless physical experiments over many decades that have proven these claims time and again with incredible accuracy. Beyond that, we have incorporated this knowledge into things we rely on every day like GPS.

GPS satellites circle the Earth and adjust themselves to the time dilation they experience due to these velocity and gravitational influences. Each satellite orbits the globe at approximately 22,000 miles and at a speed of approximately 8,400 mph. Because of that, each satellite loses 7 microseconds per day due to the velocity at which they travel. They also gain 45 microseconds due to the lower gravity of space producing a net difference of 38 microseconds gained. If they didn't adjust for these differences the satellites would cease to function properly within days and would be relegated to space junk.

Who says time travel is not possible? I learned it's too early to make that call.

SPACE BENDS

I grew up like most people, I suppose, with the perception that space was just that – space. It wasn't a thing; it was the absence of all things. Outer space was just vast expanses of nothingness except where an occasional star or planet happened along. Space didn't move, things in space moved. There was an implicit belief that every point in space was an immutable fixed point representing a universal unmoving constant.

Yoda-san held a different view. So did Einstein.

Having knowledge now of the relationships between velocity and time, and between gravity and time, it came as no grand revelation that Einstein's theory of relativity defined a relationship between gravity and space. I figure Einstein must have read a lot of Sir Arthur Conon Doyle's work. He certainly ascribed to Sherlock Holmes guiding principle revealed in book *The Sign of Four*, which is: "When you have eliminated the impossible, whatever remains, however improbable, must be the truth."

Sir Isaac Newton himself was troubled by the fact that even though he could define gravity and its behavior, he could not explain the nature of the force behind it. Einstein extended Newton's framework to recognize that while mass played an important role of gravity, there were other electromagnetic forces at play that, in comparison, were orders of magnitude stronger. These insights made it possible to begin to bridge the gap between classical physics (large-scale) vs quantum physics (small scale). These "strong nuclear forces" were nectar that enticed me to learn more.

My mind began to wander off from the lecture Yoda-san was giving. I was imagining all the possibilities of time travel, and if I had an assignment to build a time machine where would I start. What principles of relativity would I attempt to exploit? That's when Yoda-san did one of his calculated changes of vocal volume to startle me back to attention.

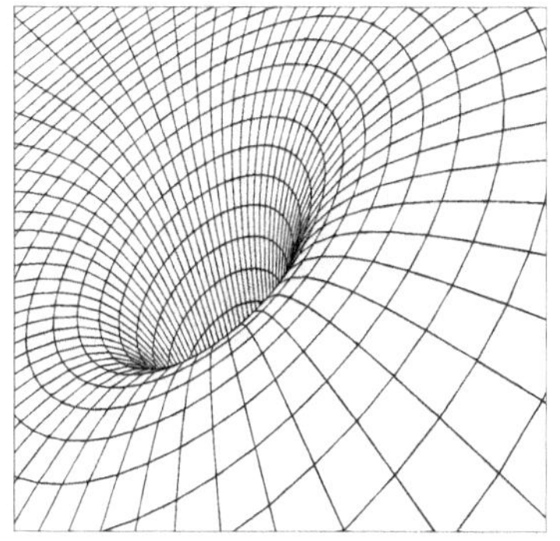

He continued to elaborate on how Einstein reasoned that "since the speed of light[5] is constant, and since we know that time dilation increases at speeds close to c, and that an observer within an inertial reference frame will experience time and distance relative to that frame and therefore for light to travel in the same elapsed amount of time relative to the inertial frame as an external observer in a state of rest, then distance – i.e. space – itself must dilate also." A very long-winded way of saying space bends.

____

[5] It should be understood that whenever the term 'speed of light' is used it implies the additional phrase 'in a vacuum'. Note also that a more appropriate term would be 'speed of any quantum particle with zero mass in a vacuum' but in the interest of brevity I will continue to just call it simply 'speed of light' or 'c' for short.

Sometimes you hear things that shake your world. Those are the things that stick with you for life. This was one of those things and it was going to come in very handy in a few years.

Meet Cheng Le

It was springtime and graduation plans were being made by all the seniors. I already had my bachelor's degree in physics and was working on my master's. I was walking with Yoda-san between his classes just to pick his mind a little about a problem I had reconciling how quantum physics seemed to contradict classical physics. He was a busy man and never had an opening in his schedule but that didn't really matter much because if you got on it there was a very low probability that he would be able to keep the appointment. His priorities were perpetually rearranging. I was fortunate because even though he was always busy I usually found a way to steal some of his precious time. Walking between classes worked best.

On this particular day as we walked north to the far campus another graduate student whom I'd seen around but never met came walking in the opposite direction. As we passed, I heard him ask without breaking his step, "How's it hanging, Yoda-san?"

Yoda-san acknowledged his presence in stride with a simple nod and left it at that. I decided I liked this guy for reasons that I fabricated out of near nothingness based solely on one inconsequential exchange. He seemed confident and self-assured with what appeared to be a playful yet respectful attitude. Beyond that, he knew Yoda-san well enough to call him Yoda-san, and more importantly, Yoda-san knew him.

"Who is that guy? I've seen him around but never met him."

Yoda-san replied, "You need to meet him."

That was good enough for me, besides, we had just arrived at his class and I had to bid goodbye. As he walked away, I thought about what he said and realized if I don't act now, I don't know when, or even if, I would ever see the passer by again. I took off sprinting after the stranger until I could see him again then slowed down to a jog.

When I caught up with him, I touched his shoulder and tried to catch my breath before announcing "Hi. This might sound a little strange and believe me that this is not a come-on, but I was just talking with Yoda-san and he told me I needed to meet you."

"Yeah, he told me the same thing about you. Apparently today is the day. Hi, I'm Cheng Le. You can call me Lee."

"Sean. Sean Blake. Hey, do you have a few minutes to talk?" I replied.

He looked quickly at his watch and said "Sure, I've got about fifteen minutes before I have to scoot. Want to talk here?" he inquired while pointing to an open space underneath and expansive maple tree. It was an unseasonably beautifully warm sunny day for this time of year so hanging outside was a welcome change from a long, wet winter.

"Perfect."

"So, what are your turn-ons?" I opened with in the hopes of showing I had a sense of humor. But once I saw his reaction I quickly followed up with "I mean, what's your major?" which on a college campus is a far safer and nearly obligatory question.

"I'm working on my master's in Electro-Thermodynamics. I've got my B.S. in Quantum Physics."

"Have you decided yet what your master's thesis is going to be about?" I asked.

"*The Impact of Strong Thermal Forces on Quantum Entanglement*" he replied matter-of-factly. I guessed he had repeated the actual title for the abstract of his dissertation. That was all I needed to hear in order to understand why Yoda-san had recommended I get to know him. He was specializing in areas I was constantly badgering Yoda-san about.

I began to share with him my fascination with quantum behavior and relativity, especially time and space warps. Without trying we kept getting deeper and deeper into the subject material. Time was flying by and we were already twenty-two minutes into the conversation. In an effort to be respectful of his time I pointed that out and asked if I was making him late for something.

"Oh, that. No, I don't really have anywhere to be. I just said that so I'd have an out if you turned out to be some self-involved geeky creep. I've got more time if you do, that is if you don't think I'm some self-involved geeky creep."

And that was the start of a life-long relationship.

ABOUT VLADIMIR KORKOV

Korkov! Premier authority on *Electron Convergence!* Brilliant innovator! One of the greatest minds of the century!

Hogwash!

O, how I detest that egotistical self-centered old-timer has-been excuse for a physicist. *'Premier authority on Electron Convergence!'* I thought to myself in disgust. Sure, he knows stuff. Sure, he's got a fascinating theory that, *if only true*, would rock the physics world. But the reality is that he can't prove it. It is just science fiction. A wonderful collection of technobabble.

"Fraud" I think better describes the man. He's as slippery as silicone and has been caught more than once publishing fraudulent claims based on questionable test results. By questionable I simply mean that he appears to be the only person who can reproduce them. For example, last May he published a paper in *The Journal of Quantum Science* about measuring the delta of strong forces before and after neutron bombardment. The results were startling and served to explain some of the remaining gaps we have in understanding quantum strong forces. The problem was that in peer review, two different physicists, a German man and a Belgian woman, attempted the same experiment as described in the article. Both arrived at similar results and neither were even close to Korkov's. Korkov to this day insists they couldn't have performed the experiment correctly. Nobody is buying his story.

"Brilliant innovator!" When I hear that my blood curdles. The man is riding on the coattails of some of the most brilliant and legitimate minds in science. He takes their ideas and claims them as his own. The science world has pointed this out repeatedly but since none of Korkov's work has been validated there are no demonstrable damages so he continues to try to ride out the storm of controversy.

'One of the greatest minds of the century!' It makes me want to puke.

MORE ABOUT LINDA

Time was flying by in school. I had completed my B.S. in Physics and was still working on my master's. Linda and I were spending more and more time together. I was convinced there was no amount of time spent with her that was too much. It felt so natural. I'd ask about her day and she would never hesitate to fill me in. She had a job, though it's a stretch to call it that, at the *Foundation for Urban Excellence* overseeing the various community projects that were mostly government funded. The big shots downtown and in D.C. relied quite heavily on the reports and opinions she generated and expressed respectively. It was shame that she was paid about what the carwash attendant got paid. She honestly didn't care. It was never about money for Linda, she was a true people-person to the core and I think she used that job to network and learn who the real players and decision makers were both locally and nationally.

In college she was working on her master's in psychology and a concurrent B.A. in Social Studies. She felt both of them were "a bunch of crap" as she would call them but she recognized she needed the sheepskins for corporate credibility. She felt that for all the studying and all the science they were grossly missing out the human element – that aspect of humanity that makes us different than other mammals and raises the expectations of how we interact. On the surface you might think she had no better insight on the matter than your typical Joe Blow on the street. Even he could tell you that "the world is completely messed up" along with phrases that began with "if I was president I would..." then never ended in anything coherent or plausible. It was different for her. She knew the world was messed up but she also *knew* how to fix it.

Linda was never that big for the physical sciences or math. Her strength was understanding people and she knew how to get herself into positions where she could exert influence. Her preferred approach was always to be the silent unseen partner.

We had been dating for a little more than a year when one day I found her in the library with a number of law books laying around the table. I couldn't help but stop. "Is this how you like to use your spare time?" I asked hoping to illicit a sarcastic response, or really any response, because I just liked talking to her.

Without looking up she said simply "Yep."

Not the reaction I'd hoped for. I should have left but I can never leave an awkward social situation until I make it worse so I furthered the one-sided conversation with "Well, let me know when you're ready because I've got a number of people I'd like to sue," confident that was going to break the ice.

She remained absolutely motionless in every part of her body except for raising her head just enough to look out over the top of her reading glasses and lock an icy stare on me. I got the message, and a smarter man would have taken his exit here but no, not me. Not my nature. One last quip before I go.

"Sheesh! You act like you're studying for the bar exam or something. I'll talk to you later." I said with a bit more snootiness than I had intended then turned away to make my too long delayed exit. Just before I was out of earshot, I heard...

"I am."

"You are? You are what?" I stopped and queried.

She sighed, sat up and pushed her chair away from the table more for effect than comfort in order to make sure I could see I had now completely broken her train of thought. "Yes. On Thursday morning I take the bar exam. If you want to go out on Friday, I think that would be great but for now, can I please study?"

I had heard what I needed to, in fact more than I planned or hoped for. I had a date. Beyond that, the timing was impeccable. I had already made some special arrangements with Willy down at the *Come on Inn.* I had a very special question to pose to Linda and needed exactly the right setting.

I bowed ceremoniously with some silly circular hand waving meant to convey gratitude and admiration but she didn't see any of it because she was already back buried in her notes. I walked away thinking *'Bar exam, huh? Fascinating.'*

CHAMPAGNE ANYONE

Friday rolled around and I was giddy with excitement. Everything was arranged. I had slipped Willy a twenty to persuade him to keep a bottle of champaign on ice for me to celebrate the occasion. He didn't have a license for booze, only beer, but it was a place that the cops knew well and knew Willy never let the bad elements hang around. They tended to look the other way for little things like this.

I stopped and picked up flowers on my way to pick up Linda. I knew that was a little risky because it was somewhat out of character for me. She was likely to be put on edge. I rationalized that maybe that would be a good thing and would create some pleasant anticipation. When I got to her house, I knocked, and she came to the door.

Wow!

She looked stunning in her red dress and wearing an imperceptible amount of makeup along with some perfume that had to be some form of aerial aphrodisiac. Her hair was perfectly arranged in a bun that exposed her neck and shoulders. She had dangling earrings that perfectly matched a modest silver necklace around her neck.

"Are those for me?" she asked after an indeterminate amount of time had passed. My jaw snapped shut and I bit my tongue that had been hanging out.

"Uh... yes," and I handed her the flowers. She invited me in so she could get a vase for the flowers. As she was filling the vase with water, and I was trying to recover by checking my tongue to see if it was bleeding, I heard her shout from the kitchen.

"I feel like doing something special tonight. How does going to Fasciano's for wine and pasta sound? I have got a real Jones for some tiramisu. What do say?"

Oh no! This can't be happening. We have to go to the *Come on Inn* tonight. It's the plan. I already bought the champagne! I had to think fast and I could come up with nothing that could trump tiramisu at Fasciano's. '*Quick... think of something.*'

"Hey that sounds great, but it's Friday night and we don't have a reservation. I doubt seriously that we'd be able to get a seat." Hmm... Pretty good, that might just work.

"Yeah, you're right," she said disappointedly, then immediately perked up. "But you never know. I'm going to call them and take a shot." Then without hesitation she pulled out her phone and speed dialed the restaurant before I could utter a word, not that I had any words to utter.

"Hi, is there any chance of a party of two getting a reservation for tonight?" she inquired then waited for the answer. "You're kidding!" she exclaimed. "I didn't think we had a shot. Thank you so much. We'll see you at 8:30 then. Thanks again. Bye." Then turning to me she announced, "They had a late cancellation."

My world was crashing down. How could that happen. Fate is supposed to be on my side tonight. Then it occurred to me, it's only 7:00 now, there's lots of time between now and 8:30. There's a chance still.

"What extraordinary luck," I managed to say rather unconvincingly. "Hey, would it be OK if we stopped by Willy's on the way? Willy owes me five dollars because the Lakers beat the Nuggets last night." I hated to use a bald face lie but extraordinary circumstances required extraordinary measures.

"Sure, that works. I like Willy."

Phew! Disaster averted. I'm back in control and the plan is back on.

We got to the bar and I immediately relaxed. I was back in my element. Luck had turned my way because I saw Linda's usual table was unoccupied (if I had been thinking I would have had Willy save it). No matter, it was vacant so we made our way over while shouting to Willy, "Two porters please." He acknowledged with a wave and we sat down – I was careful to make sure my back was to the stage. Willy brought our drinks and left. Linda and I engaged in some friendly chatter while I quadruple checked that the ring was in my pocket. I don't know what we talked about because I was rehearsing my song to make sure I remembered the lyrics. I did however notice Linda was getting antsy because she kept checking the time on her wristwatch. I finally realized the time was now or never.

"I've got a very special question I've got to ask you. Sit right there and I'll be right back," I said.

She fidgeted in her seat a little and with a hesitant voice she said "Oh Sean... are you... are you sure you want to do this right now?"

"Oh yeah. It's definitely time. I'll be right back." With that I got up, went onto the stage, and grabbed my guitar. I didn't use any amplification and just sat on the edge of the stage right next to Linda. I then proceeded with my overly rehearsed revamped version of *Linda, oh Linda* that had won her heart a year ago.

Linda Oh Linda
My Little Buttercup
Linda Oh Linda
You got me all messed up

Linda My Linda
You're the best thing in my life
Linda Oh Linda
Will you be my wife

I put the guitar down and moved closer to her while pulling out the ring and presenting it to her. I waited... and waited... before she broke a beautiful smile all the while crinkling her forehead and grabbed my hand, closed the ring box, and whispered "I am <cough> blessed."

THUD!

That was the sound of my heart landing on the cold hard tile floor. What the hell did that mean? I knew her well enough to know I didn't get an answer. She didn't say yes or no. She didn't answer. What in the hell does that mean?

"Oh, crap, look at the time. We better get going. It's almost 8:30" she said.

So, we got up and began to walk out. I looked up at Willy and he gestured quizzically by extending his open palms and raising his shoulders as if to ask, "What about the champagne?" I returned the same gesture and followed Linda out the door.

It was a long, silent ride to the restaurant. My head was reeling and I was trying to save face by not making a big deal about it. We got there and our seats were ready as promised. We sat down and waited for the waiter to come.

It wasn't long before a well-dressed man in formal attire approached our table and announced, "It is normally our custom to ask if you would like anything drink while you peruse the menu but tonight, I understand is a special occasion."

Yeah, it was supposed to be special occasion but that went up in smoke about twenty-five minutes ago. *'Wait a minute...'* I thought, she never mentioned anything about a special occasion on the phone. *'What the heck is he talking about?'* I wondered.

He continued "So tonight we're doing things a bit differently." As he spoke two other waiters arrived at our table, one with a huge slice of tiramisu and the other a chilled bottle of champagne. He set the tiramisu quite purposely in front of me so I could read frosting laced words.

"Of course I will," it read.

The other waiter removed the champagne bottle (it was the exact same brand that was now getting warm under the bar back at Willy's) and taped to the bottle was a twenty-dollar bill with a note that read "Congratulations Sean." It was signed "Willy".

Bewildered I looked at Linda and she gleefully said, "I paid Willy fifty bucks to rat you out. He's got a little integrity so he's returning your bribe and champagne. Now, show me that freaking ring you gorgeous hunk of man you."

2. THE END OF THE BEGINNING

> *Only those who attempt the absurd*
> *can achieve the impossible.*
> Albert Einstein

IT'S ALL RELATIVE

I loved both quantum physics and all the incomprehensible possibilities that had huge potential in the real world. But that love was dwarfed by my fascination with time and interstellar travel. Linda had a hard time understanding my fascination with what to her appeared to be nonsense – warping space and bending time – but she legitimately wanted to understand it at some cognitive level before dismissing it.

It was that interest that one day prompted her to ask, "So why is it called the *Theory of Relativity* as opposed to something more like the *Theory of Spacetime* or *Theory of Probabilities*? I mean, is there a twenty-five-words-or-less description of relativity you could tell me that doesn't have all the techno-speak but would give me a rudimentary understanding of what fascinates you so much?"

"I don't know about twenty-five words or less, but I'm certain I can explain the term 'relativity' in three minutes or less." I was relishing the thought of summoning my inner "Yoda-san" and explaining a highly complex subject in very understandable terms. "And if I do my job right, when I'm finished, you will ask to go a little deeper, say, on the order of a one-hundred-fifty to two-hundred-words-or-less level of description."

"Let's just play it by ear and start with the simple three-minute description first, OK?"

Game on! This would be the true test. Einstein's own words were flying through my brain which was raising the stakes – for me anyway. He once said, "If you can't explain it simply, you don't understand it well enough." If I couldn't explain it simply enough for someone as intelligent as Linda to understand, then I clearly didn't have a firm understanding myself.

So I began, "Excellent. So, to explain this we'll use what Al would have ..."

"Al?" she interjected.

"Yeah, Al, as in Albert, as in..."

"I got it... continue," she interjected again only with a playful exasperation.

"I was just trying to keep my word count to a minimum," I mumbled as an explanation before continuing. "Anyway, *Mr. Einstein* liked to examine things using what he called "thought experiments" so that's what we're going to do. Here's how it works.

"First, imagine a man, we'll call him Jack, standing in front of a railroad car that is one hundred feet long. It has a wall on the front end of the car. Jack is just going to observe and measure things. Got it?"

"Got it," she confirmed.

"Ok. Now a woman, we'll call her Jill, gets on the train car and she has a tennis ball she throws at the wall of the car from twenty-five feet away. It takes exactly one second for the ball to return to her – in other words, a ball velocity of fifty feet per second, but that's not really important yet. So now, what did Jill see? I'll answer that for you. Jill saw the ball go twenty-five feet, bounce off the wall and come back twenty-five feet in exactly one second." Then I followed with, "And what did Jack see?"

She sheepishly responded, "That the ball went twenty-five feet then back again in one second?"

"Ah, grasshopper, you make me proud," I acknowledged making an obscure reference to a long-forgotten TV series about martial arts and inner self awareness.

"So, Jack and Jill saw the same thing. Now, imagine that the train car is traveling at one hundred feet per second – about seventy miles per hour – and Jill does the same thing, throws, and catches the same ball. What did she and Jack see, or in better terms, experience?"

Again, Linda sheepishly responds using the exact same verbiage ostensibly thinking that if it worked twice, it should work again, "That the ball went twenty-five feet then back again in one second?"

I replied with sympathetic disappointment, "I'm afraid not. That is exactly what a smart and intuitive person such as yourself might think, but incorrect, and yet at the same time, also correct, depending on your perspective." Her silent scowl told me to continue quickly or I'd find myself sleeping on the couch tonight.

"What I mean is, from Jill's perspective, you are absolutely right, she saw the ball travel twenty-five feet out, then twenty-five feet back, all in one second. She didn't see or experience any difference between the bounce when the train was stationary versus the bounce when the train was moving. According to her *relative* frame of reference all measurements of time and distance were the same. But from Jack's *relative* perspective on the ground, one half second after Jill threw the ball, the train, Jill, and the ball had all traveled fifty feet forward due to the velocity of the train alone. In another half second the train had traveled another fifty feet, and the ball, now back in Jill's hands was one hundred feet farther down the track from where it was originally thrown. So, who's measurements are correct,

Jack's or Jill's? Did the ball travel fifty feet like Jill measured? Or did it travel one hundred feet like Jack measured?"

With pensive irritation she stated, "This had better not be one of those ridiculous yes or no questions where the answer is both yes and no."

"They BOTH are!" I regrettably exclaimed before I had allowed her last response to sink in. "Here's another way of thinking about it. You're driving down I-90 going seventy miles per hour. Four hours later you know you have gone two hundred eighty miles. But to an alien who lives on the sun observing you, remember this is a thought experiment, you are travelling at 67,375 miles per hour – the speed required to circle the sun in one year plus the seventy miles per hour you're driving – observes you traveling more than a quarter million miles. So, you see, Einstein reasoned that everything we observe and experience is *relative* to our frame of reference, hence the term 'relativity'. Cool, huh. Are my three minutes up?"

Ignoring my question she responded, "Ok, connect the dots for me now. I get the rationale for the term 'relativity' now, but how does anything you said relate to warped space or bending time?"

I'm thinking, '*Good job, Sean. You answered her question and she wants to go deeper.*'

"I'm so glad you asked. Here's where it gets a little weird and more complicated but it's worth it. Are you game?" I asked.

"Let's try. You get three bonus minutes."

"Make it ten," I countered.

"Four."

"You drive a hard bargain... Seven. Final offer! Take it or leave it." I negotiated emphatically.

"Three."

"Let's not quibble, four minutes it is," I conceded in order to put an end to the haggling and move on before she could counter-offer. Besides, I knew I wanted this more than she did. "But first, just for clarity, let's review a couple of things you already know – and these don't count as explanation time."

Playing along she asked, "Ok, what do I already know?"

"You already know that velocity, distance, and time are all related and each is defined as a relation of the other two. For example, velocity is defined as the speed required to travel a distance of thirty miles in a time of one hour – that is thirty miles per hour. Similarly, distance is how far you can go at a certain velocity for a given amount of time. Same for time. Simple right?"

"Yes, quite simple. What else do I already know?"

"You also already know that nothing can travel at or faster than the speed of light, right?"

"That is also correct," she confirmed before looking at her watch and adding, "Your four minutes starts... Now."

"Ok, here we go. Hold on to your seat. This is going to get weird and wonderful. Let's go back to Jill on the moving train." I then parenthetically added, "By the way, in physics we would refer to Jill on the moving train as the 'observer in an inertial frame of reference' and we would refer to Jack on the ground as the 'observer in a reference frame at rest', just in case you want to sound really smart at a party sometime."

"Oh, thank you so much. I'm sure I will use that as an ice breaker at my next social gathering," was her sarcastic response.

"Ok then... back to Jill... the moving train... We'll use the same experiment only this time we'll observe velocity instead of distance. So, this time as Jill passes by Jack, she throws her ball forward and Jack sees the ball travelling one hundred fifty feet per second – the hundred feet per second from the train *plus* the fifty feet per second additional from her throwing it. Likewise, if she throws it backwards Jack sees it traveling at fifty feet per second – the train's one hundred *minus* the throw of fifty. Still tracking with me?"

"Yep, that's all pretty intuitive," she confirmed.

"Now the fun part. Take the same exact scenarios only this time instead of a train we have a spaceship, and instead of a tennis ball, we use a light beam from a flashlight. Now imagine that the spaceship is 93,000 miles long – the distance light travels in one half second – and Jill puts a mirror on the front end. The spaceship is stopped in space and not moving. Facing forward from the end opposite the mirror, she turns on her flashlight and one second later the light beam returns after reflecting off the mirror. No different than the tennis ball example with the train stopped; no space warping; no time dilation; just what we expect. Agreed?"

"Yep. So far, so good."

"Now the spaceship starts traveling at ninety percent of the speed of light and Jill turns on her flashlight emitting the light beam. Once again Jill sees the beam of light reflect back exactly one second later – just like the moving tennis ball experiment. But this time there's a difference. The tennis ball example would teach us that the light beam should be moving forward at the speed of the spaceship plus the speed of the light beam, right? But, as you already know, that is impossible because *nothing* can travel faster than the speed of light. Likewise, when she turns backwards and turns on the flashlight, one would intuitively reason that the light should be traveling at the speed of the light beam *minus* the speed of the spaceship. But again, not so.

"No, the fun aspect of light is that it *always* travels at the same constant speed, in all directions, regardless of the speed of the inertial frame of reference! Isn't that so cool?" I probably should have waited with the "so cool" line until I was finished but I could tell her attention was fading and I needed to pull her back in, and her tone of voice with her next question confirmed that.

"And any minute now you're going to get to the point of the original question, right? What does that have to do with warping space and bending time?"

"It has to do with this. We know Jill saw the beam return in exactly one second because that's how long it took when the spaceship was stopped. Just like the tennis ball experiment, it doesn't matter whether moving or stopped. But the difference is, in the tennis ball example, the speed of the tennis ball varied with the speed of the train. With the flashlight example the speed of the light beam is constant – the speed of light. So instead of the light beam hitting the mirror one half second after starting, it doesn't because the mirror is no longer where it was when Jill turned the flashlight on.

"Since the spaceship is travelling away from the light beam at nine tenths the speed of light – that is 167.6 thousand miles per second – the light beam after one half second is still 83.7 thousand miles away from the mirror. If you do the math... You trust me on the math, right? If you do the math, you find it will take the light beam five full seconds to catch up to the mirror. And it still needs to make the return trip – which, by the way, only takes about one fourth of a second – so something has to give. And since the speed of light is an immutable constant, then the thing that has to give is distance or time or, as is the case here, both. I told you it would get weird and wonderful. How am I doing?"

"Not there yet, and you've only got sixty seconds left."

"That's all I need because contrary to what you might think, all the math gets much simpler than what you deal with in everyday life. Remember our earlier discussion of the relationship between velocity, distance, and time? If you are going thirty miles per hour you'll go thirty miles in one hour, but if you need to go sixty miles then you need to either travel twice as fast or have twice as much time – or one of the infinite number of combinations of the two, like traveling forty-five miles per hour for an hour and twenty minutes for example.

"But when we are talking about light speed it all gets way, way simpler. First of all, light travels at light speed always; never faster; never slower. Second of all, the formulas for time dilation and length contraction show that the two change together in proportion to the velocity of the spaceship. So instead of endless possible combinations of variations of distance and time, for any given velocity there is one mathematical answer for both. Here, look at this..." I said pointing to my computer screen. "You don't need to be a mathematician to be able to see that both of these formulas for time and length, t and l respectively, are based on the same relationship of light speed and velocity, c and v respectively.

$$t = \frac{t_0}{\sqrt{1 - \frac{v^2}{c^2}}}$$

Time Dilation

$$l = l_0 \sqrt{1 - \frac{v^2}{c^2}}$$

Length Contraction

"So, wrapping it all up we must conclude that in order for Jill's observation of the light returning in one second to align with Jack's observations of the reflecting light taking over five seconds, Jill's time had to have slowed down. Similarly, Jill's distance the light beam travelled had to have contracted proportionately to align with Jack's observations of more than five times that distance.

"So, there you have it – space warps and bends; time dilates and slows down. And if you can bend space, I say you can bend time. And I intend to prove that someday.

"So, what do you think?" I concluded.

She closed with, "I think I'll stick with people and the real world and let you deal with your Jacks and Jills and the space time continuums."

WHICH WAY TO GO

More decisions had to be made now that my graduation was at hand and I would need to reenter the real world. The same was true for Linda but to a lesser degree because she always lived in the real world, to her it wasn't just a place to visit.

I was more fortunate than so many others that struggle with what to do next. I wasn't working from a blank slate and wasn't concerned with *what* I would do so much as I was concerned about *which one* I would do. Linda always knew she would make the world a better place so her decision was really only *how* to accomplish it.

Linda and I discussed this weighing pros and cons, debating relative and actual benefits and all those things that are important in choosing one's life path. She always expressed unwavering confidence in whatever I would choose. As much as I liked the idea of intergalactic travel and, dare I say it, time travel, I just couldn't find any real justification for going that route. Together we agreed that, while fun and challenging, it would only serve to satisfy geeky scientists and entertain the world's billionaires. There seemed to be no real practical applications on which it would be worth spending time. So, we decided to go down a different path together.

Quantum Construction is what we termed it. Linda had already gone through the process of getting the term trademarked. *Quantum Construction*, or QC as we called it, had unlimited potential including plenty of near-term opportunities with huge benefits as well as immense potential in the long term for humankind.

What is *Quantum Construction* you might ask?

Imagine a process whereby we tap into the incredible wealth of energy that exists in every single particle of matter – the strong quantum forces that hold everything together, the quarks that make steel strong, water pour, ice cold, rubber bend, and glass shatter. What if you could use that energy to direct and coerce atoms to bond to each other naturally in ways not currently found in nature. Imagine a process that would create a substance lighter than aluminum, stronger than steel, entirely clean to manufacture, cheap to produce and limited in application only by the imagination of humans. I could draw an analogy to Green Lantern's ring in the right hands but that is fanciful fiction. What we intended to bring to the world would be well founded in scientific fact.

The potential benefits would be massive and easy to predict. What would be less easy to predict would be the collateral damage that would result in this type of process if it was mishandled. For every hour we spent thinking about what we could accomplish with a process this powerful, we spent five hours discussing the pitfalls and unintended side effects that were inevitable from this kind of 'progress'. We were acutely tuned in to those aspects and were of unified mind that our guiding principle had to be of the same substance as the first law of the medical profession's *Hippocratic Oath* best summarized by "Primum non nocere" or "First, do no harm."

Admittedly, Linda was the one that kept me focused on the humanitarian aspects. I agreed whole-heartedly with her but it just wasn't always in the forefront of my thinking. I on the other hand had to constantly remind Linda that regardless of how humanitarian I was, I had no intention of living like a pauper for the rest of my life. I did not require extravagance and wanted none of the problems of the filthy rich, but I certainly wanted enough money to pursue our shared interests without having to beg venture capitalists for money and permission to do it. Fortunately, *Quantum Construction* could certainly generate more than generational wealth. Learning how to control and manage it would hopefully be a fun problem to have.

THE SEED OF AN IDEA

Now that we had direction it was time to pull things together and, to use one of my favorite phrases, "gitter done." To that end we invited Lee to the house one Saturday afternoon to share our thoughts and aspirations and see if it was something he could embrace or if he thought we were just crazy. We knew it could go either way but we also knew that by the end of the day he'd either be in or he'd be out. It turned out to be a much harder sell than I anticipated.

The first half hour was more of a sales pitch than anything else. Linda started by painting a world where financially challenged countries would have a scalable sustainable way to manufacture common items that currently were imported at costs prohibitive to the average person. Just simple things like water troughs and feeding bins at first. Then later, fences for livestock which they currently don't have. She moved through a gamut of examples: bridges that could be constructed in weeks instead of years; road surfaces impervious to salt and weather that never have potholes; earthquake proof frames for skyscrapers that would be thinner and stronger that anything known to man. The list went on and on.

Cheng Le was amused but not sold. There were too many unanswered questions. I could see we should have started with the science and backed into the benefits.

I took over and attempted to reach him by talking to his strengths. Unfortunately, his strengths were my weaknesses, which was what made it so appealing to get him to work with us. I started on topics we had already talked about countless times in our discussions over the past few years and eventually got to the heart of the matter – the directed bonding of hadrons that makes the dream possible.

I started, "I believe it is possible to coerce, no, bad choice of words, *direct* certain atoms to bond with other atoms in exactly the same way they do in nature but also to get them to do it in combinations that have never been done before. If done with design, intent, and insight we can create the compound that will suit our needs. We start at the end by defining the desired characteristics then follow that with the analysis as to the molecular combinations that cause those characteristics. For example, what makes steel strong and aluminum light? When we have the answer, we design an element with the appropriate atomic weight then overload the outer electron shell with valence electrons such that the particles will *want* or rather *need* to share its elections with the other elements of our choosing forming the desired outcome."

"Cool concept, in theory, but I'm not seeing much science in what you're saying, just a lot of optimism. What makes you think you can *direct* isotopic elements to bond in ways that nobody else has ever been able to do? You speak of overloading the outer shell of the atom but as you are well aware that is simply not possible. Every electron is bound by the limits of its shell's capacity. Nature dictates the phases of the electrons in each orbital. Trying to change what nature already dictates is fools play. What am I missing?"

"I wouldn't call it "missing" but what you haven't considered yet is that this becomes almost trivial if we discover a new element of our own design. We don't break any rules of quantum mechanics, we work with them," I said with a satisfying tone of voice eagerly waiting for him to take the bait.

"That's a pretty ambitious achievement. Exactly how do you propose accomplishing that when the periodic table has been completely filled with every possible atomic weight balancing the exact number of possible electrons against the positive forces of protons in the nucleus. There is simply no room for anything else."

"I'm talking about *ununennium*, in a way."

"But that's nothing but a theoretical element. It's never been discovered or even generated in a lab. It's just a name for a non-existent thing – a placeholder in a non-existent row in the table. And need I remind you that every single one of the elements we have been able to create, the entire f-block, are all unstable and radioactive," he replied with defiance I had been anticipating.

Group →	1	2	3	4	5	6	7	8	9	10	11	12	13	14	15	16	17	18
Period																		
1	1 H																	2 He
2	3 Li	4 Be											5 B	6 C	7 N	8 O	9 F	10 Ne
3	11 Na	12 Mg											13 Al	14 Si	15 P	16 S	17 Cl	18 Ar
4	19 K	20 Ca	21 Sc	22 Ti	23 V	24 Cr	25 Mn	26 Fe	27 Co	28 Ni	29 Cu	30 Zn	31 Ga	32 Ge	33 As	34 Se	35 Br	36 Kr
5	37 Rb	38 Sr	39 Y	40 Zr	41 Nb	42 Mo	43 Tc	44 Ru	45 Rh	46 Pd	47 Ag	48 Cd	49 In	50 Sn	51 Sb	52 Te	53 I	54 Xe
6	55 Cs	56 Ba	*	71 Lu	72 Hf	73 Ta	74 W	75 Re	76 Os	77 Ir	78 Pt	79 Au	80 Hg	81 Tl	82 Pb	83 Bi	84 Po	85 At	86 Rn
7	87 Fr	88 Ra	*	103 Lr	104 Rf	105 Db	106 Sg	107 Bh	108 Hs	109 Mt	110 Ds	111 Rg	112 Cn	113 Nh	114 Fl	115 Mc	116 Lv	117 Ts	118 Og

*	57 La	58 Ce	59 Pr	60 Nd	61 Pm	62 Sm	63 Eu	64 Gd	65 Tb	66 Dy	67 Ho	68 Er	69 Tm	70 Yb
*	89 Ac	90 Th	91 Pa	92 U	93 Np	94 Pu	95 Am	96 Cm	97 Bk	98 Cf	99 Es	100 Fm	101 Md	102 No

"Absolutely correct. But what if it wasn't just theoretical. What if we created it?" I paused for effect and to allow time for him to reflect on that statement. "Of course, we wouldn't call it *ununennium*, that's almost as bad as *berkelium* or *californium*[6]. We could call our element *lenium* with an atomic symbol of "Le", you know, named after you. We could consider *chengonium* if you like, but that's even worse than *berkelium* and *californium*." I added with a playful smile.

Nope. No reaction whatsoever, just pensive thought. He could always tell when I was patronizing him.

---

[6] These elements have atomic weights of 97 and 98 with atomic symbols of Bk and Cf respectively as depicted in the table.

I continued, "Look at it this way, we already know the characteristics that residents of the currently non-existent eighth row will have – the atomic weight, number of atomic orbitals, etc.   Using *field quantization,* we have infinite degrees of freedom for the quantization of the electromagnetic field. I'm not saying I have all the answers, in fact I'm insisting I absolutely do not have all the answers, that's why we need you onboard. If this is possible, I will need your expertise in quantum electromagnetism. There's a very reasonable probability that I'm wrong, but you have to admit, there is also a slim chance I'm not crazy brain-dead loco."

"Hmm..." I heard him utter on the verge of surrender. Time for the closing argument as Linda would say.

"And you know better than I that 'whatever is not forbidden...'"

"is compulsory," he said completing my sentence.

"And 'whatever can happen...'" I added.

"must happen," he concluded.

"Do me a favor and think about it over dinner," I said knowing full well that he was intrigued enough that he couldn't not think about it. "Linda made some shrimp lo mein to help woo you. Let's eat then Linda has some more stuff we have to discuss before you make any decisions. There are some other things you must wholly buy into if we're going to work together."

BRINGING IT ALL TOGETHER

The dinner was relaxing and satisfying. Everyone made a point to get away from the heady discussions we had been having all evening and instead, talk about trivial things like sports or the weather. Topics like politics and current events were never brought up. Occasionally, out of the blue, Lee would blurt out some random question. I had learned that it worked well to rephrase the questions slightly then redirect them back to challenge him to answer his own question. This had the effect of making him act as if he was already part of team even though he had not yet committed.

"How can we ever be sure that these new particle entanglements won't slip out of phase and completely collapse?" he asked.

I replied, "That's a question prototyping will answer for us. If you were to guess, what would you think the best approach should be for electron phase stabilization?"

Then a little later, "Do you have demonstrative evidence that compound molecular bonding can be achieved at large scale with stability?"

"Yes, and no," I responded with a certain predictability. "No, I don't have that evidence now, that is not yet, but yes, in that I will assure you that this project proceeds only when 100 percent certainty regarding stability at any scale is achieved. There must be zero margin of error. Zero!" The redundancy was for emphasis. "I read your thesis and was intrigued by your concept of quantum energy conservation. Do you think there could be an application of your theories with regard to molecular bonding?"

When everyone had had their fill, I started collecting the plates and gave a little nod in Linda's direction. Linda acknowledged the signal and unceremoniously changed the subject while we still sat at the table.

"There are some other things that we alluded to earlier that I want to go over with you. You need to be 100 percent on board on all of them or it is a deal breaker. I have absolute faith in you and Sean and I know with absolute certainty that you will identify all potential paths of technical failure and eliminate or mitigate them. My role is to identify then eliminate or mitigate those non-technical issues that are inevitable with success. Wherever there is technological progress it is accompanied by money which in turn invites power and greed. Therefore, in order to ensure the true success, we must take absolute control of all three, money; power; and greed. Compassion will be our guiding principle, 'It is only progress when everybody wins' is our mantra. So, here's the plan..."

With that said Linda laid out the simplified high-level four-point plan into which she had put countless hours of thought. To those who would think this overtly simple plan did not warrant the effort she had spent on it, I would simply remind them of the axiom used in computer science, "Writing complex code is hard. Writing simple code is even harder."

The plan:

1. Sean Blake maintains complete and absolute control over all any and every technical aspect of the project.
2. Linda Blake has absolute say on the rate at which this technology is rolled out into the world.
3. All committed investment funds are placed in advance in an escrow account controlled by us and disbursed as needed.
4. Investment monies will be distributed in the following proportions: 35 percent will go toward the science side – equipment, supplies, wages, etc.; 65 percent will go toward social causes to prevent and alleviate the potential harm – lost jobs and other psychological traumatic effects that always accompany change.

She concluded with, "Do you see anything in there that you can't live with?" then waited patiently giving Lee all the time he needed to mull it over. In her mind, the longer he took the better. It was an indication he was giving it his full attention.

"I've got some questions. First, I want to say I personally have no issue with any of what you laid out. I have all the faith in the world that you and Sean have a grip on reality and a sincere heart for mankind. I am just massively skeptical that you will ever get the corporate world to agree to those conditions. This is going to take a boatload of money to pull off, on the technology side alone. Allocating two thirds of the finances to ancillary causes seems improperly skewed but frankly, as long as 35 percent works for the tech I'm happy," said Lee then pausing to formulate the follow-on to his statement.

After a polite period of time Linda questioned, "And second? You had questions?"

He replied, "Yeah. Let's assume that we are wildly successful and our tech is getting used worldwide. You and Sean will not be able to maintain that kind of control indefinitely. It just won't scale. What is the plan for transitioning control out of your hands into somebody or something else?"

Excellent question Linda thought while she formulated her answer. She was also pleased with the observation that he had used the phrase "our tech". She figured he was no longer sitting on the fence but rather was firmly on her and Sean's side. Now he was just taking a final look at things to decide whether or not he should jump back to the other side.

"Let me explain it this way. In society and the human psyche, everything plays together and a small change here and there has ancillary effects downstream, not that different from the science world you know so well. I know there are an infinite number of potential outcomes but we only have to deal with the one outcome that will happen. Therefore, we must ensure we get the outcome that is best. I wish there were axioms and indisputable truths and universal constants in the social/psychological world like you have in yours but there are not. But I believe in the human spirit. That is why we must guide this project with an unshakeable moral compass and uncompromising convictions. That is how we win.

"Let me paint the scenario I believe is not only the best outcome but also the most likely. We start small, very small, in fact tiny. The world will be skeptical and we need to prove ourselves in a non-threatening way. As they can observe the successes and start to see the value they will relax and we will start to do larger and larger projects. Small incremental projects with relatively proportioned value. Soon there will be pressure to go faster, faster than would be healthy, so that's where we *throttle down* the progress while regular people get new training for new jobs. Eventually, over years and years, critical infrastructure gets replaced with permanent materials not requiring maintenance. For example, roads are indestructible so governments don't need as many tax dollars. Many consumer products are cheaper to produce therefore cheaper to buy. Taxes drop, commerce expands, people start doing more of what they want rather than what they need. Inflation actually reverses into deflation – how's that for a concept? Once all this is accomplished and the pattern is established, it would be foolish for anyone to say, "Let's do it different now." It simply wouldn't be allowed to happen. So therefore, the problem of transition becomes infinitely more manageable and predictable."

There was another one of those long reflective pauses but this one was going just a bit too long.

"So…?" Linda prodded.

Lee leaned back in his seat, placed his palms on his thighs, then looked across the room at me and said emphatically, "Damn! She… is… good!" which broke the tension in the room that had been building. He then looked back at Linda, then me, then Linda again and said "I'm in. Let's do it."

THE EARLY STAGES

With very limited funds we proceeded to prototype and experiment with the process. We relied heavily on the good graces that both Lee and I had earned at the university. We exchanged guest speaker dates for time with the particle collider. Our early experiments were just exploring what was possible regarding atomic bonding and what was not. We had no real end goal other than to gain knowledge. Some of our first results, while not marketable in any way, were incredibly important to our learning. Here's just a few:

- There was the fragile elastic substance made from molecularly rearranged copper. It was expensive to make without much utilitarian value. We called it our $174 rubber band.
- There was chalk that couldn't be erased.
- We made a wire that was lightweight and strong with virtually no electrical resistance, but it got corroded by coming in contact with literally anything, including insulation – it could only exist in a perfect vacuum.
- One we put in our back pocket for later was glass that allowed light to pass through only in one direction. It had the effect of a one-way mirror but worked on a different principle.

The more we experimented the more we learned. The more we learned the more defined our actual approach became. We worked this way with little money and fewer tools until one day our ship came in, well, more like a dingy but we received a small government grant that Linda had applied for months prior. It was just a couple of hundred grand but that enabled us to get some much-needed lab equipment and take the next step in our exploration.

With this new influx of money, my thoughts started to gel on an approach. We started with a spreadsheet of the various elemental properties of the periodic table. We mapped atomic number, density, boiling point, melting point, in short, any and every property of interest.

| | | | | | | | List of chemical elements | | | | | | | | |
Atomic number	Symbol	Neutron Count	Name	Group	Period	Block	Standard Atomic (Da)	Density (g/cm3)	Melting point (K)	Boiling point (K)	Specific Heat Capacity (J/g·K)	Electro-negativity v	Abundance on Earth (mg/kg)	Origin	Phase at Room Temp.
69	Tm	99	Thulium	n/a	6	f-block	168.93	9.321	1818	2223	0.16	1.25	0.52	primordial	solid
70	Yb	103	Ytterbium	n/a	6	f-block	173.05	6.965	1097	1469	0.155	1.1	3.2	primordial	solid
71	Lu	103	Lutetium	3	6	d-block	174.97	9.84	1925	3675	0.154	1.27	0.8	primordial	solid
72	Hf	106	Hafnium	4	6	d-block	178.49	13.31	2506	4876	0.144	1.3	3	primordial	solid
73	Ta	107	Tantalum	5	6	d-block	180.95	16.654	3290	5731	0.14	1.5	2	primordial	solid
74	W	109	Tungsten	6	6	d-block	183.84	19.25	3695	5828	0.132	2.36	1.3	primordial	solid
75	Re	111	Rhenium	7	6	d-block	186.21	21.02	3459	5869	0.137	1.9	$7{\times}10^{-4}$	primordial	solid
76	Os	114	Osmium	8	6	d-block	190.23	22.61	3306	5285	0.13	2.2	0.002	primordial	solid
77	Ir	115	Iridium	9	6	d-block	192.22	22.56	2719	4701	0.131	2.2	0.001	primordial	solid
78	Pt	117	Platinum	10	6	d-block	195.08	21.46	2041.4	4098	0.133	2.28	0.005	primordial	solid
79	Au	117	Gold	11	6	d-block	196.97	19.282	1337.33	3129	0.129	2.54	0.004	primordial	solid
80	Hg	120	Mercury	12	6	d-block	200.59	13.5336	234.43	629.88	0.14	2	0.085	primordial	liquid
81	Tl	123	Thallium	13	6	p-block	204.38	11.85	577	1746	0.129	1.62	0.85	primordial	solid
82	Pb	125	Lead	14	6	p-block	207.2	11.342	600.61	2022	0.129	1.87 (J+)	14	primordial	solid
83	Bi	125	Bismuth	15	6	p-block	208.98	9.807	544.7	1837	0.122	2.02	0.009	primordial	solid
84	Po	125	Polonium	16	6	p-block	209	9.32	527	1235 –		2	$2{\times}10^{-10}$	from decay	solid
85	At	125	Astatine	17	6	p-block	210	?	575	610 –		2.2	$3{\times}10^{-20}$	from decay	unknown
86	Rn	136	Radon	18	6	p-block	222	0.00973	202	211.3	0.094	2.2	$4{\times}10^{-13}$	from decay	gas
87	Fr	136	Francium	1	7	s-block	223	1.87	281	890 –		<0.79	$\sim 1{\times}10^{-18}$	from decay	unknown
88	Ra	138	Radium	2	7	s-block	226	5.5	973	2010	0.094	0.9	$9{\times}10^{-7}$	from decay	solid
89	Ac	138	Actinium	n/a	7	f-block	227	10.07	1323	3471	0.12	1.1	$5.5{\times}10^{-10}$	from decay	solid
90	Th	142	Thorium	n/a	7	f-block	232.04	11.72	2115	5061	0.113	1.3	9.6	primordial	solid
91	Pa	140	Protactinium	n/a	7	f-block	231.04	15.37	1841	4300 –		1.5	$1.4{\times}10^{-3}$	from decay	solid
92	U	146	Uranium	n/a	7	f-block	238.03	18.95	1405.3	4404	0.116	1.38	2.7	primordial	solid

I wrote an Excel macro that looped through the table data identifying all the various combinations of element nuclei that when added together would produce and element with an atomic weight of 119, 122 or 126, at least to start with. I chose these values because they appeared to be the most probable to produce an element with the characteristics we needed based upon analysis of existing elements and their characteristics.

Here is the over-simplified essence of my strategy.

In the days before quantum physics, it was generally believed that the driving force that held atoms together was gravity. Protons and neutrons have mass, electrons do not. The mass of the nucleus generated gravity that was responsible for holding the nucleus together while electromagnetism was the force that kept the electrons in their shells, subshells, and orbitals. With the advent of quantum physics, we learned that there are two more nuclear forces at play, we call them simply *strong nuclear force* and *weak nuclear force*. The fantastic part of the discovery is that of the four now known forces holding our universe together, gravity is the weakest of the bunch – by a LOT!

- Weak nuclear force is 10^{25} stronger than gravity
- Electromagnetism is 10^{36} stronger than gravity
- Strong nuclear force is 10^{38} stronger than gravity

That translates into the strong nuclear force being **1,000,000,000,000,000,000,000,000,000,00 0,000,000,000** times stronger than gravity!

My thinking was that if we could find a way to 'borrow' just a teensy-tiny amount of that power for just a teensy-tiny amount of time before returning it, then do it billions and billions of times in succession, the possibilities of what we could accomplish were limitless. I needed Lee to validate the concept and agree so I explained my thinking to him and asked what he thought.

"Fascinating idea, but I don't see how you would get around the *first law of thermodynamics*[7]?" was his reply.

"I'm not talking about creating or destroying energy, only borrowing it. We indisputably know that the amount of energy in the universe is constant, and we also know that energy can be changed, moved, controlled, stored, or dissipated," I said. "Einstein's formula, **E = mc²**, tells us there is a direct relationship between mass and energy. Consider that even though c^2 is a big number it is, nonetheless, nothing but a number, a conversion factor if you will. So, what it tells us is that energy IS mass, only with mass multiplied by a constant. It's analogous to kilometers and miles, both kind of the same thing with different names. If I want to know how many miles 10 kilometers is, I multiply 10 x 0.621 to get 6.2 miles. I can go the other way by multiplying miles times 1.609 to find that 10 miles is 16.1 kilometers. Same thing. We can change energy to mass and vice versa the same way."

"Other than a remedial high school physics lesson, where are you going with this?"

"Hang with me here," I pleaded, "I'm almost there. Would you agree that our biggest hurdle is finding a way

---

[7] The *First Law of Thermodynamics* states essentially that neither matter nor energy can be created or destroyed.

to combine the nuclei of various atoms into a single nucleus with a cumulative atomic weight?"

"Yes. That would be the plan and that would take a tremendous amount of energy to accomplish." As a point of emphasis he added, "Tremendous!"

I responded, "Exactly! That's the energy I want to borrow. We can coerce the valence electrons to quantum leap from their current orbital to an inner one, *temporarily*, and capture the emitted energy for our use. The *Balmer Transition* tells us each electron that jumps from, let's say from orbital three to orbital two, will produce a photon of red light with an energy of 1.89 eV. Then we take that cache of energy and use it to get the nuclei to collapse together. Once that happens, the cumulative nuclear strong force from all the source atoms should necessarily force the affected electrons into the appropriate, phase-compatible orbital." Now, here's where I figure it's going to get interesting because I don't have the answers to the questions that I know are coming.

Lee then questioned, "My quick math tells me that the total number of electrons of all of the source atoms is going to necessarily create an orbital count that exceeds all of the orbital counts of all the source atoms. You'll need more energy for them to move the outermost level. Where are you going to come up with that?"

"I don't know. That's where you come in. You're the expert on energy conservation." I thought the direct approach would be best.   I'm pretty sure he's not convinced yet because his verbiage "you'll need" and "where are you…" indicate he's not owning the problem yet. So, I asked the follow-on question, "Do you think that when the nuclei combine there might possibly be an emission of nuclear strong force that we could use?"

After a reasonable amount of time for thought he answered, "Yes and No," with a grin. "Yes, there might possibly be an emission, and no, but that would be very unlikely. What you're asking for is impossible."

"And?" I asked in a very drawn-out enunciation of a single syllable.

"And…" he mimicked in that same drawn-out enunciation, "you know what big Al says, 'Only those who attempt the absurd…'"

"'Can achieve the impossible.'" I concluded for him.

"OK, what the heck. We've got some government money to burn, let's give it a shot."

Pitching the Idea

I had very mixed feelings about our upcoming encounter with the corporate world. I was dreading the need to deal with the starched-collar pencil necks that I needed to convince to give us boatloads of money. But a man's got to do what a man's got to do. And I had to do this. Normally I enjoy explaining complex concepts of quantum mechanics to an unenlightened individual but that is only fun when said individual is interested learning something foreign to their way of thinking. It is an inescapable fact that quantum mechanics is foreign to everyone's way of thinking. My experience with corporate big shots, however, was that there is very little you can tell them. And if it is something they can't imagine, something they could never have thought of, then you're really wasting your time.

"Should I wear a suit and tie?" I asked Linda.

"No, definitely not. You need to be you, you know, a little bit off center but likeable and smart. In fact, I was thinking you should have a pocket protector and a slide rule hanging from your belt." was her playfully ornery response.

"Thanks, but no thanks for the help." I pouted.

"Oh relax, you'll be great. I'll open it up and pitch all the benefits we have to offer and paint mental images of stacks of money laying on a table just asking to be snatched up. These guys can never resist that kind of talk. Then you come in and dazzle them with all your technobabble which they will have no ability to comprehend but they will nod knowingly in order to make them feel like they are very visionary. To cap it off, I swing in while they are still in their fanciful stupor imagining what color their next yacht will be and pass the hat, collect the checks, and we scoot on out of here. Easy peasy."

"Well, when you put it that way..." I facetiously acknowledged.

"But seriously, really, you'll be great. Just remember to exude confidence. Your presence has to translate as 'I've got something you need and I'm here to lay it on you!' Be overtly polite but never condescending, and always ask if there are any questions," I was instructed. "These kinds of guys like to show how smart they are."

"That's always the hard part for me, the Q & A part. It always demonstrates how little they comprehended of what I said. Just once I would like to get an intelligent legitimate question, but instead, they always come across like a sixth grader asking some obvious question not out of curiosity but just to get a good grade in class participation."

We finished getting dressed and double checked that we had everything we needed loaded on Linda's laptop. Linda had some printed handouts with some of the high-level concepts outlined which really are not intended to be informative but rather served the purpose of a business card with all of our contact information: address; phone; web site; and email. She wants to build a relationship not necessarily answer questions. I didn't have to load up my demo equipment because it was already in the trunk where I put it the previous night before coming home from the lab. Once ready, we headed to the venue.

We arrived in plenty of time to get the laptop plugged into the projector which displays on a massive wall behind an enormous stage. The room, now empty, was an auditorium that seated about three hundred people I guessed. It was way bigger than I expected. I was glad to see we had generated that kind of interest. *'Maybe this wasn't going to be too bad after all,'* I thought.

As we got closer to the starting time people started straggling in, eight people in seats and about four others still concluding their conversations. I checked my watch and rationalized internally, "There must be some long-running meeting going on somewhere. I hope it ends soon." About one minute later the lights dimmed and man in suit and tie went up to the podium and began to introduce the special guests.

'What the hell is this? You can't be serious. That's it, twelve people for a room that seats three hundred?' I found myself muttering under my breath. I suddenly felt deceived. I was looking forward to speaking to a large crowd, reminiscent of lecture classes for 100 level classes back in college.

My mumbling was interrupted by the words, "So would you please welcome Dr. Linda Blake," followed by meager applause from ten of the twelve people present.

Linda was standing next to the MC so she was at the podium immediately. That served to make the feeble applause less obnoxious in my estimation. Linda was not flustered at all, at least if she was, she never let it show. I needed to take lessons from her, so I silently practiced feigning excitement so I'd "exude confidence" when my turn came. After a quick introduction and opening slide, she progressed quickly to her key PowerPoint slide which she would refer to for the next fifteen to twenty minutes.

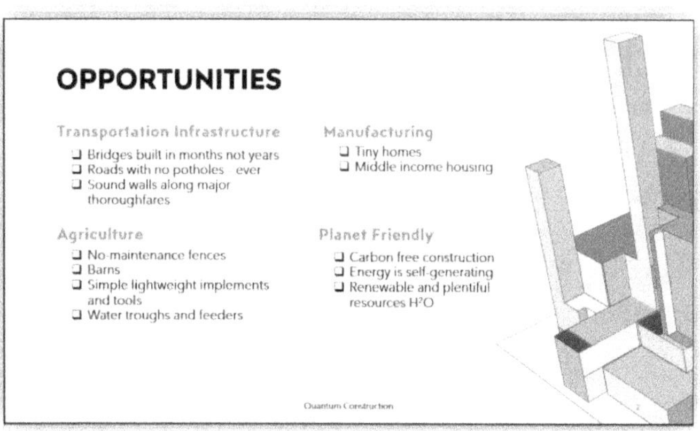

I noticed she skipped slide number two and went straight to number three. With grace and charm, she stepped through the slide, elaborating on the key benefits of the proposed technology. She spoke nearly twice as long on this one slide than normal. I was a little concerned that she would lose the audience if she spent that much time on each of her four other slides. They were the slides that would touch on the strategy of slow rollout and all the other humanitarian aspects the got her excited. Then she stunned me. Without ever flipping to another slide, she announced to the room...

"Now let me introduce my partner – in more ways than one – and the President of Blake Industries," she began, then, in an obvious move to give me more time to collect myself and get up to the stage, she continued to uncharacteristically ramble on about my accolades. "a doctor of Quantum Mechanics, author of three groundbreaking papers published in *The Journal of Quantum Science,* professor of electrodynamics and spare time, wannabe time-traveler, Dr. Sean Blake!" There was of course a round of phony obligatory applause.

I walked on stage and she met me well away from the open mic on the podium and touched my hand while whispering "Keep it short or you'll lose them."

I quickly whispered back "Blake Industries? Professor? You really stretched the truth with that one."

"We needed a company you could be president of. And you 'profess' that stuff all the time. Did you think I meant something else?" she smiled.

I made my way to the podium while thinking *'That explains why she didn't use her last four slides.'* I was already deciding what I was not going to cover. I decided to pare down my presentation to just two topics, then I'd go to the dreaded Q & A which I would now intentionally and thankfully cut short.

"Linda says I'm a wannabe time traveler. Well, that might be true but what she doesn't mention is that given the profession all of you present have chosen I'm fairly certain that you are time-travelers and just don't realize it." A very slight but audible murmur from two audience members could be heard which was better than dead silence. I continued asking rhetorically because I knew this wasn't the type of crowd that would actually respond to any questions, "Would I be wrong assuming that each of you has, at some time, taken a jet across country or overseas? If so, then you were to some degree time-traveling." I went on tell the story of the Hafele-Keating airplane experiment with the cesium clocks.

"So, you see, fantastic things are not only possible but do in fact happen regularly in daily life. Furthermore, that in order to fully comprehend the quantum-based science you are about to hear about, you need to open your minds to consider things that years of education have taught you are not possible." I didn't think I made an impression, but that could be because my attitude about the venue sucked. I hearkened back to Linda's advice and bolstered up some more confidence and politeness.

"Let me show you a small example of the technology that we're currently developing. This is a form of a proprietary compound we're currently developing called Trilenium Quadra Chloride." I held up a baseball sized ball of what looked like clay for all to see. It wasn't really TQC but they didn't know that. "Pretty unexciting, I know. Not really much different than Play-Doh. But let me show you something amazing."

I walked off to a table on stage that had a box twelve inches by twelve inches by twenty-four inches. It had a cord going to an outlet but the audience couldn't see it because a curtain concealed it from site. I split the ball into five equal pieces then rolled them out into the shape of a five-inch pencil. I held them up for all to see, much like a magician performing a trick, then placed them in the box. "Now, ladies and gentlemen," I announced as if I was a barker at the state fair, "behold what happens when exposed to very targeted beam of specially formulated gamma rays..." I clicked a button, a light flash occurred and I reached into the box, removed the five pencil-shaped objects, and began passing them around the room for examination. I let the audience deal with having to actually get up and walk to the next person given everyone was scattered in the rows of seats. One person on my far right waved off the woman bringing him a pencil effectively saying, "Don't bother."

While they were looking over the non-functional pencils, I explained the details of the billions upon billions of molecular transformations that just happened then estimated the amount of atomic energy that was generated and conserved. It all fell on deaf ears. Now I had to confess to the room that I tricked them.

"In fairness I need to confess to you that what you are holding in your hands is only a simulation of the final product. What you just saw was a simple magician's trick. The box on the table is really just a box with a light bulb. If I were to bring the actual TQC transducer, we would have required a venue even larger than this one, and they don't easily fit in the trunk of a car." I joked. I was relieved to hear a few chuckles, so I thought, '*OK, here's where I cut things short and end on a highlight.*'

"Now I'd be happy to answer any questions."

"Can you make a pencil that actually writes?" came from someone on the right.

"No, the lead that makes pencils work is soft and scrapes off onto other soft things like paper. This compound is stronger than steel."

"Can you make a computer with this stuff?"

Remembering Linda's advice, I politely replied, "No. I won't say it isn't possible but electronics is not a focus right now. I don't see that happening in the near future. Any more questions?"

"Can you make a carbon-free alternative to gas?" coming from the attendee closest to me.

Now I'm thinking to myself, *'Right. Gas that's stronger than steel and lighter than aluminum. PA-LEASE get me out of here!'* but I politely reply, "No. And to save time I'll mention there are limitations to every process. The technology won't make flowers or fabricate rib-eye steaks either. Think in terms of hard impervious surfaces. Anything else?" I ask in order to quickly move on.

"I'm no physicist but I was taught in high school that matter can be neither created nor destroyed. Are you saying that law does not apply to you?"

I paused thoughtfully, probably longer than I should have, but that became moot when I involuntarily blurted, "You are absolutely right. You're no physicist."

Needless to say, that didn't win over the minds of anybody in the room. All that time preparing, wasted. Linda was staring daggers at me. I had blown it.

The man that served as the MC tried to smooth things over and told Linda they would talk things over and get back to us next month if they decided to pursue it.

She checked her calendar and replied, "It will have to be sooner than that. We pitched this in Denmark earlier this week and are on our way to Frankfurt, Hyderabad, and Beijing in the next ten days to do the same. We acknowledge this isn't a good fit proposition for everyone and we thank you for taking time out of your busy day for us."

"Silent" is not a word I would use to describe the ride home. "One-way" and "unidirectional" both work. She talked, I listened. I couldn't do that again, ever.

Forming the Consortium

Excitement was building and the world was beginning to visualize the vast potential of our process. Even though we didn't have a product yet, everyone wanted a slice of the pie and the big players kept vying for the whole pie – they didn't want to share. They were under the mistaken belief they could just outbid the competition and get what they want. That was never going to happen. Linda would never accept a "one winner takes all" scenario. Already the big guys were making deals, bad deals, with the smaller players that had no chance of taking the grand prize. Contracts were being written where the little guys would be paying extorted prices for the tech. They were sold that it was a "good deal" compared to current costs, but their cost was to be double or triple what would be fair. In addition to all of that the whole process of travel, pitches, and negotiations was wearing her and me down.

"You know, I've been thinking. Our current approach for finding investors isn't working very well, we need to change things up a little," she said.

"In what way?"

"I think I've got a way to offload all the coordination of contracts to an outside entity and yet still maintain complete and total control. I want to create a consortium of investors as a legal entity with a charter, by-laws, all that stuff. You and I then deal exclusively with that consortium."

"How does that protect our interests?" I replied.

She went on to explain, "I'll be the one writing the charter, by-laws, and operating procedures, all of which will directly embody all of our requirements. The by-laws will be written in such a way that modification will require the unanimous approval of the board and all partners – meaning us, we are the only partner. Of course, we will not be able to actively participate on the board or daily activities in order to avoid even the appearance of conflict of interest. You've seen what's going on right now, the rich and powerful are already making power plays to have exclusive rights and preying on those that can't compete with them. We can't allow that."

"What makes you think you'll be able to get anyone to participate in such a closed system?"

"Because" she began, "it's all predicated on greed and power. Once the world knows that the consortium is the only entity we will deal with, the little guys are going to buy in immediately. They will see it as relief from those horrible agreements they are currently making with the bullies. Once they are committed it won't take long for the others to join because if they don't, they get left in the cold."

"Masterful!"

Moving on she said, "Here, take a look at this," and she handed me a single printed PowerPoint slide. "If you want more detail than viewing at the twenty-thousand-foot level I could show you the pages of legal documents I've prepared."

I nodded appreciatively and said, "No, PowerPoint is good."

"What I gave you is just the directives, if you want to see the mission statement and charter, I can show you those too," she added.

"This is fine." With that I took a look at the slide.

OPERATING DIRECTIVES

Participation

- Any entity that agrees to the *Terms of Agreement* can participate in the group
- Participation with The Consortium does not provide 'ownership' of any kind in *[insert our name]*
- Any entity may voluntarily terminate their participation at any time, including *[insert our name]*
- Any entity investing an amount greater that 15% of the mean participation rate must provide a commensurate amount to the Equity Pool

Return on Investment

- Profitability is limited to 20% gain over expenses
- Any entity investing an amount greater that 15% of the mean participation rate must provide a commensurate amount to the Equity Pool
- Entities that can provide evidence of hardship are eligible to extract funds from the Equity Pool
- Work will be provided in this order:
  - ✓ Need based
  - ✓ Value added
  - ✓ By quorum constent of The Consortium

Quantum Construction

"Let me ask, what is the 'Equity Pool' you reference?"

"The equity pool is a mechanism to prevent the big guys from squelching the little guys. Anyone attempting to increase their overall percentage of investment will need to also throw some cash into the proverbial hat that can be used to help those entities, mostly countries, more financially strapped. I've still got some work to do there but I'm confident it can work."

"Also, you have references to 'insert our name' in a couple of places. What's that?" I followed with.

"That is something we need to talk about right now. We can't just keep saying 'our project' or making up names on the fly any longer. We have to come up with a legitimate corporate identity."

I replied, "Well you'll be glad to learn I've been giving considerable thought to this. I'm still flexible on the final name but I do strongly insist that it have the word 'Enterprise' in it, like *Prime Directive Enterprises* or *Vulcan Enterprises*. Got any ideas?"

"Perhaps something that better reflects who we are and what we do would be better, something like *Quantum Construction Enterprises*," she said with a certain finality.

"You've already trademarked that, haven't you?" I asked helplessly.

"Yep."

"OK, that's cool. I like the name. Now, what do you think about this. Every day at 5:05 PM we're required to take a coffee break in '10-Forward'."

"Why 5:05?" was her puzzled response.

"Because that's 1705 in military time." I announce triumphantly.

"Yeah...?"

"Linda, I'm disappointed. You don't recognize the starship Enterprise's call letters - 'NCC-1705'?"

She ended the discussion with, "I think this is going to be harder for you than you think."

Thus was formed *The International Consortium of Industrialized Nations and Entities for the Advancement of the Human Race* or ICINEAHR for short. You can see why we just referred to it as *The Consortium.*

Linda Meets Marissa

One Saturday Linda was working with the *Helping Heroes Help Themselves* non-profit agency to structure agreements with local builders and businesses to provide at-cost labor and supplies for the construction of housing for disabled American veterans. A team of students from the Computer Science department had volunteered to spend the day setting up the networking infrastructure, pc's, printers, and other assorted technology at the agency's headquarters. One of those students was Marissa Faraday. She was younger than most of the students at her level.

Linda noticed right away the respect that Marissa commanded from the other students which made her glad she was there. Now Linda had a single point of contact for all that stuff she didn't know much about and didn't have to answer techy questions she wouldn't have answers to. Marissa was handling all of that. At one point Marissa had questions for Linda about some network topology and layout and the mutually agreed they should find a table or desk somewhere and draw some pictures.

As they were getting things figured out, they engaged in polite chit chat as most people would. Marissa asked Linda about her background and how she got involved with *Helping Heroes Help Themselves*. Linda shared her passion for people and her philosophy of life. Marissa commented she thought that was all admirable and that maybe, someday, she too would get more involved. But she also mentioned her intentions that day were not so much charitable as they were practical. Her day was going to count as credit toward some Social Sciences assignment and besides, it got her out of the classroom for a day. Linda felt Marissa needed to see how her talents and expertise were helping those who truly needed it.

"Come on, I've got someone I want you meet," and Linda grabbed her hand to lead her to an office down the short hallway.

Along the way Linda asked Marissa about her studies and what she was majoring in to learn that Marissa was into hydrological chemistry and computer science. Networking was simple and natural for her and quantum computing had captured her imagination.

They arrived and the office door was open. At the desk was a heavy-set friendly woman who upon seeing Linda, rose and embraced her in a bear hug. There was a quick exchange of pleasantries before Linda made the introductions. "Roda, meet Marissa, Marissa... Roda. Marissa is the tech expert that's getting your network in."

Roda responded, "Very pleased to meet you, Marissa. I can't tell you how grateful everyone here is for your help." Then noticing Marissa's transfixed eyes on the prosthetic that served as a replacement for her right arm from the shoulder down she quickly summarized the story like she had done countless times, "Iraq. IED."

Linda then said to Roda, "We won't take much of your time but I was wondering if you would share your story with Marissa." Marissa picked up this was not the first time these two had this same conversation. Roda told Marissa about the war, the explosion, and all that led to and how Linda had helped her find the appropriate help for dealing with the trauma, both physical and mental. She pointed out how life changing the acquisition of the prosthetic and how it was all due to kind people like her.

Marissa cried. Linda smiled.

As they walked back down the short hallway Linda said to Marissa, "You told me what you're studying but I want to know what you're passionate about, they often times are not the same."

"Yes, that's true, at least in my case it is. I'm studying what I'm studying because it is marketable but I really have a passion for history and those people who took the time to record things so others later could learn about them. I'm talking everything from the cavemen that wrote on walls, to those that wrote on papyrus scrolls, to the folks today that record video and blogs. It is fascinating to me."

"Really." Linda replied not as a question but more an acknowledgement of understanding.

"Yeah. Think how cool it is for the authors of the dead sea scrolls, for example, to know that their work would be read centuries after they were long dead. That's just cool to me."

Linda was beginning to entertain thoughts of introducing her to Sean wondering if she had any expertise that might be useful for *Quantum Construction Enterprises*. Given her age she doubted Sean would have much interest. But then, Marissa made another comment that changed things.

"Another thing that I find fascinating right now is the work a guy named Vladimir Korkov is doing with nuclear cohesion. Have you ever heard of him?"

"I've heard a little, not much," she replied, downplaying how much she had heard Sean tirelessly complain about him.

"It's just that I think he's brilliant and really misunderstood. He's got this theory that he's so close to proving but just can't. The science world is rejecting him but I think he'll be vindicated. I can't articulate exactly why but I think he's on to something.

'Oh, I've just got to introduce her to Sean. That will be so much fun.' Linda thinks. So, she asks if Marissa would like to meet Sean, which of course she does since Sean is well known on campus for his brilliance in quantum physics and computing. She then confides in Marissa about Sean's attitude toward Korkov and asks her to play along. When they meet, would she please go heavy on the accolades for Korkov and how mistreated he is.

Marissa smiles and says, "Sure, I can do that. Sounds like fun."

SEAN'S FIRST 34TH BIRTHDAY

From a vacation cabin in the Southern Cascades in the Great Northwest, on my 34th birthday, I'm on the deck watching the clouds settle into the valleys between the rolling hilltops. Above the clouds are the snowcapped peaks whose snow line is rising, imperceptible to human observation but rising nonetheless. While I am always struck with awe at the sheer visual splendor of God's work on a grand scale, likewise I have also learned to appreciate the marvel and majesty of the quantum world encapsulated in a single cubic millimeter in the tip of each cloud where the mist seems to magically mutate over time into nothingness. Sheer natural unseen beauty at the other end of the scale.

It's 6:30 AM PDT, August 24 in the year 2060. After a grueling eight and a half years of research, experimentation, writing, review, and rework I'm celebrating the completion and publication of my signature paper *Time, Space and Quanta – Interactions that Challenge Relativity*. I apparently had forgotten to cancel my daily reminder to check my iChron[8] for my running to-do list for the day. I sincerely tried to not look while I cancelled the alarm because Linda would be disappointed if she found me working while on vacation. I couldn't help seeing the list was blank. That made me feel better and I put the device down while powering it off.

Soon thereafter I got pleasantly surprised by the scent of hot hazelnut coffee wafting onto the deck. I looked up and saw Linda carrying two cups and wearing one of my t-shirts. I couldn't tell if she had anything on underneath, but I learned long ago that reality is not a prerequisite to enjoyment, so I just envisioned what I wanted to. It worked. My birthday was improving by the minute.

---

[8] An iChron is an unreleased product I was beta testing – a personal assistant with audio, video, and augmented reality.

She came over to me, leaned down and whispered "Happy Birthday" in my ear with that indescribably sensual voice she is able to turn off and on, then gently kissed me on the lips. She held it longer than I was expecting but got no complaints from me. Then, upon seeing my iChron (thank goodness it was turned off), she picked it up and placed it way outside of my reach on the table next to her lounger while saying (in her not-so-sensual tone of voice) "You know, it's your birthday and we're on vacation. That's two reasons you do not have a to-do list today." She then came over to my lounger, sat on my lap with her legs straddling the lounger and looked me straight in the face. With that first voice she whispered in my ear "Do you need a third reason?"

Then with one deft uninterrupted movement she solved the mystery of what was under that t-shirt.

MARISSA JOINS THE TEAM

I was working in my office when Linda got home and entered through the front door shouting, "Honey, I'm home. Where are you?"

I shouted back, "In my ready room."

Linda turned to Marissa and explained, "He insists on calling his office his 'ready room'. Do you get the connection?"

"Fancies himself as a Jean Luc Picard does he?" she replied. Linda was relieved she didn't have to explain it to her.

She and Marissa walked through the house to my office and entered. I sensed her presence and without looking up asked vacantly, "How did it go?"

"It went great! There was a lot of help and we got everything installed and tested. It's all working perfectly and there's no reason to go back tomorrow. But hey, turn around, there's someone I'd like you to meet."

I took off my reading glasses, stood and walked over to Marissa to greet her while Linda made the introductions. "This is Marissa. She was an incredible blessing to us today. She took care of all that TCP checkbitting and RCP stuff for us. Now all the office computers can talk to each other." I did not correct her flagrant abuse of the technical terms.

"Pleased to meet you Marissa, sounds like you were needed today."

"Thank you, Mr. Blake," she replied. "Linda exaggerates a little, it was a team effort and it was educational and fun."

"Call me Sean. Mr. Blake makes me feel old. Let's go to the living room and sit and you can tell me how you two met. Would you like a drink, soda, or iced tea?"

"No thanks, but don't let that stop you," she answered.

Once we were seated Linda and Marissa summarized their day and explained how Marissa got out of class to help. After that, Linda started to tout the laurels of Marissa's acumen for quantum physics and quantum computing. It had just the effect she hoped for and expected. I sat up and my attention level went up a notch from polite to interested.

"So, what aspects of quantum physics are you studying? What floats your boat?"

Marissa recognized the setup was complete. It was time to lay it on and lay it on heavy. Linda was already smiling.

"I guess in addition to all the normal mainstream stuff, right now I'm completely taken up by the fascinating work a guy named Vladimir Korkov is doing on electron convergence. Everything I've read by him I find absolutely mind blowing. That man has forgotten more than I could ever hope to know about nuclear cohesion. I truly believe he is right on the verge of proving a theory of his that bridge the gap of understanding between classic Newtonian physics and the world of quantum." Marissa gushed. Now Linda thought this was all play acting but the truth was that Marissa actually did believe in his work and that Korkov was on to something big, at least 90 percent of her was sure. She also knew there were some gaps she couldn't fully understand but was confident he would figure them out.

Sean decided to take the high road and brow beat her with scientific logic instead of emotional ridicule. "Well how can you have that position when it is well known that his research is flawed, his concepts are incomplete and peers seem to be unable to replicate his results using his test methods?"

She replied confidently, "I concede his research is incomplete as of today, but that's true of everyone right up to the day it is complete. And as for his peers, I've read the dissertations by Edwards and Hodges about not getting the same results as Korkov. But I looked thoroughly into how they interpreted his findings and approach and I tend to side with Korkov that they missed some important aspects of the test."

"Like what?"

"Well, for one, Edwards stated that since the nuclear cohesion force was immensely stronger than gravity, it would be redundant to sample both electromagnetic cohesion as well as thermodynamic cohesion. He missed the fact that Korkov's approach accounts for changes due to the observer effect and that by not performing the second set of tests, once could never hope to produce those same results. Hodges similarly discounted certain parts of the test regiment. It makes me wonder who tests the testers? You're an accomplished coder so I'm sure you've written software and unit tests confirming it is performing perfectly only to turn it over to QA who rejects it due to some failed test. You spend time looking for a nonexistent bug before you look at the test code and find it was the test itself that was flawed not your code. Same thing."

I was actually a little taken aback by that well thought out response. I knew she was spot on with the coding example and also knew I had never thought to question Edwards or Hodges methods. I thought to myself, *'I kind of like this girl. There's something about her.'*

Linda jumped in to break the silence with, "Well, I can't speak for you guys but it's late and I'm hungry. Marissa, would like to stay and have dinner with us?"

I echoed the sentiment, "Yes, please stay for dinner. You've worked hard today and I'd like to talk a bit more. What do you say?"

"Thank you. I'd be honored to be your dinner guest," she replied with a small curtsy and ingenuous smile. "Linda, is there anything I can help you with?"

"If you're talking about helping prepare dinner, talk to Sean about that. It's his night to cook," she replied.

"Oh crap!" I exclaimed having just remembered something. "I asked Lee over tonight to go over atomic weight calculations."

"Just invite him to dinner. Then he can meet Marissa too."

That was a perfect arrangement. I knew Linda and I were thinking on the same lines. It would be expedient for Lee to meet Marissa sooner rather than later.

Not too long later Lee arrived, we exchanged introductions and since supper was ready, we all sat down to eat. Lee and I started talking science, and algorithms, and postulates, and such. Normally, Linda would have discouraged that at the dinner table but tonight was different. Besides her being outnumbered three to one by scientists, she wanted to watch how Marissa interacted with the other two, much older, much more seasoned men.

At one point Lee was lamenting the amount of time he wasted that afternoon trying to get the neuron laser integrated with the control console.

Marissa asked, "What are you using for the subnet mask on the local network? The usual 129.*.*.10?"

"Probably. Is that something I need to worry about?"

"Not normally, but a lot of highly sensitive test equipment like to talk RPC instead of TCP. In those cases, since you're already behind the outer firewall, you can just drop the mask or use "*.*.*.*" instead."

Lee looked around the table and asked both Linda and Sean, "Where did you find this woman. I think I like her."

Linda and I exchanged eye contact across the table and we both knew the other was thinking the same thing. We had the team we needed. It would take a few days to formalize the arrangements and ensure everyone was onboard.

PREPARING FOR THE BIG ONE

We had been in negotiations with *The Consortium* for fifteen months now. They were hugely reluctant to accept the costs Linda insisted they bear to deal with the inevitable side-effects of the project. They were also very irritated that we would exclusively control, or should I say throttle, the rate at which we rolled out the technology.

"OK, this is it. This is what we've been working towards. Are you ready?" Linda asked me as if we hadn't been discussing this solidly for years. Her tone of voice seemed uncharacteristically filled with trepidation which meant for the first time I was beginning to feel some anxiety about "the meeting".

"I'm ready, but something seems to be bothering you this morning," I casually replied in an effort to open the discussion without creating any additional stress. I continued, "Would it help to go over the plan one last time before we go in? After all, this is your world and I'm just there for moral support for the most part." She agreed that would be a really good idea and thankfully took the lead in this conversation to go over the minutia. She then became far more assertive and started to repeat to me the talking points and critical success factors we had discussed at nauseum no less than a thousand times already. I didn't mind because I could tell it was already restoring her self-confidence and giving her that calming *"I'm in control now"* feeling which is exactly where we both needed her to be.

"One. I do all the talking and I control any part of the business side of the conversation. You will be there to speak to technical issues only. Check?"

"Check." I replied.

"Two. We will not agree to any scenario in which you have anything less than 100 percent control over any and every technical aspect of the project. Check?"

"Check." I confirmed.

"Three. All investment funds will be paid in full in advance or at minimum placed in escrow thereby assuring us that a threat of withholding funds cannot be used later to apply pressure to change any of the aforementioned parts of the agreement. Check?"

"Perfect." I replied getting excited all over again at the prospects of what we were on the verge of accomplishing.

"Four. You acknowledge this is a pure business meeting. It is not a brainstorming session. We are not demoing anything. We are not going to entertain new requirements. This meeting is strictly finance and compensation. Are we clear?"

"Crystal." I proudly replied showing I was listening closely and could alter my response in context with the question all the while starting to wonder what the real reason was for why we were going over this "one last time".

Then she paused and I was certain it was not out of hesitancy but for effect. She hadn't yet acknowledged that we were done so I *knew* we weren't done. Linda never left loose ends. I racked my brain trying to remember what all we had talked about and what I had forgotten that would have her so nervous just prior to the biggest meeting of our lives.

"There's one last thing…" she began ominously, again pausing for effect before continuing "and I apologize for waiting until now to bring this up." Bingo! We had finally gotten to that one last all important item that was stressing her out. "You need to agree with this or it's a deal breaker. This is not negotiable and I will resign from this company in a heartbeat if you don't comply. Understand?" I could find no words. I'm pretty sure my jaw was slowly dropping because every ounce of brain power I possessed was searching for an answer to an as of yet unasked question. I could feel the muscles in my arms, legs and neck involuntarily tightening. Thankfully, my silence was properly interpreted as confirmation of agreement so she could conclude uninterrupted.

"No lemon meringue π jokes!"

It took a while to set in but it didn't take her long to begin jumping around like a sprinter running in place while seemingly punching a nonexistent punching bag in front of her after which she stood upright and motionless, pointed a finger at me and proclaimed "You've been punked! Admit it. I got you!"

No argument there. She got me. I bit... hook, line, and sinker. Surprisingly, I felt absolutely no anger as one might expect simple because the relief that was flooding over my body completely overwhelmed every other emotion. That is when I realized that her little prank was in fact not really a prank, at least not in spirit. It was a well-planned tactical maneuver intended to calm *me* down prior to going into an incredibly important setting which I would not control. It worked masterfully.

THE BIG ONE

It was 10:15 AM and we were on the road. The office building where we would meet with *The Consortium* was not far from our home.   We would be there in approximately fifteen minutes for a meeting scheduled for 11:00 AM. I was on autopilot and Linda was driving, both physically and metaphorically. She was in her element and in complete control from this point forward and I couldn't have been happier. She took the time to explain to me the sequence of events that I should prepare for prior to and during the meeting.

"We should get there about thirty minutes early so we might need to go for a cup of coffee or something before the meeting. We will arrive at their office at 10:54, that is six minutes early showing we're prompt and dependable but we don't waste our time frivolously. Remember, these guys are professional well-educated lawyers and they do this stuff every day. They have their tricks and tactics and they will use them. If I knew what they were I'd tell you but I don't. Don't worry about it, just trust me. I've got this."

'*You've got this.*' I thought to myself in a reassuring tone of thought while I tried to wipe the sweat off my palms before she noticed. That was the conversation-ending phrase we used which conveyed 100 percent certainty that things were under control and no amount of conversation can possibly change that.   It was understood that a single misuse would render the phrase meaningless so it was used sparingly.

She stopped at a stoplight for just a few seconds before it turned and we started to go again. She then asked, "By the way, did you grab the draft contracts off the desk?" I think I shrieked "What?" as my body convulsed. She started to chuckle until she had time to take her eyes off the road and glance at my painfully distorted face. "Oops... sorry. That was taking it a bit too far. I'm sorry." She sounded sincerely apologetic and continued in a convincing and consoling tone, "For the record, I've got them. Relax. I promise, I won't do that again."

I accepted her apology then reached in the back seat and grabbed her briefcase. Making no attempt to hide my actions I opened it up to visually confirm that the draft contract was indeed in there. What I found surprised me. There was not just one draft contract but a number of different ones – four to six different ones was my guess. I knew they were different and not just copies because the number of pages in each one varied. They also had what appeared to be a color-coded piece of tape on each one. I asked her what that was all about and she smiled smugly and replied "It's contingency planning. Depends on how the negotiations go as to which copy I pull out."

She recognized my bewildered "Huh?" look and continued.

"You don't want to see me pull the red one out. That means things went as bad as we might have feared. Orange, better but not good. Blue is OK but Green is our target – that's the one I'm hoping to get to use. Yellow is better than expected and gold is, well, self-explanatory."

I was constantly amazed at how well she understood a world I could not even begin to comprehend.

"I'm expecting that they are going come on strong right out of the gate with a nebulous offer meant to sweep us off our feet. Do not react. We're going to let them think they did sweep us off our feet. At the end of the day, it's all just talk until it's backed up in writing. That's where it gets easy because then everything is known and quantified. Capisce?"

I acknowledged "Capisce."

As we pulled into the parking garage, she put a note of finality to our conversation stating, "And remember, I do the talking."

The receptionist was a modestly good-looking woman in her 40s with a pleasant and professional demeanor. She acknowledged our presence and offered us a beverage which we declined. She announced our presence and less than a minute later a tall well-dressed man came out of the board room and enthusiastically greeted us saying "Glad to see you made it. Everyone is already inside. Come with me." I couldn't help but think to myself *'Glad to see you made it. Right. Like there was any possibility in the world that we would miss this meeting.'* We hadn't even sat down yet and I was already railing on the lawyer. I was so glad my instructions were to keep my mouth shut.

We entered the room and politely shook hands with each member of their team while exchanging introductions. They had two attorneys and two finance folks present along with the CEO. I knew he was the CEO by way Linda zeroed in on him. She had an innate talent for discerning the real decision makers. Once all the pleasantries had been exchanged and the second offer of beverages had been declined, we sat down at the conference room table. I noticed that nobody took a seat at either end of the long narrow table, a clear sign they were trying to make us feel comfortable and on an equal plane with nobody sitting in the power chair. I intentionally slid my chair seven to eight inches away from Linda to create a noticeable separation making it clear to any idiot present that I was going to be as silent in these proceedings as their CEO was almost certain to be.

Once everyone was settled and before there was any sort of pregnant pause the man named Charles, the obvious brain trust and chief negotiator, opened with "Sean, Linda... We'd like to make you billionaires. What do you think?"

BOOM! Talk about coming on strong. All I could think of, besides Linda's instructions to me to not react, was '*Oh, you poor bastards. You have no idea who you are dealing with.*' She had their number before they even opened their collective mouth. I coyly looked in Linda's direction while gently scratching a non-existing itch on my nose to watch how she handled it. With just exactly the right amount of hesitation, a very controlled smile came to her face indicating she was pleasantly pleased but falling just short of being giddy. She replied calmly with a precisely measured amount of excitement, "Wow, that's fantastic. This meeting is going to be over sooner than I anticipated. That's exactly the kind of number we were hoping for as a starting point. Are you willing to put that in writing?"

I had no idea this meeting was going to be so entertaining. I looked around the table taking note of each individual's reaction. One accountant looked worried; the other lawyer looked pleased like a hunter watching his prey take the bait. The CEO didn't flinch. I could tell by looking at Charles, who registered absolutely zero emotion of any kind, that he was processing her statement. I'm fairly certain that he was the only one at the table that noticed those four words in the middle – "as a starting point." He was trying to figure out what she said. Did she just agree or was she just starting negotiations? Should he pull out his draft contract for us or would that be tipping his hand way too early. He looked like a deer in the headlights of an oncoming bus.

"Of course we would, but would you mind clarifying what you meant by 'as a starting point'?"

Change of serve. He just "passed the hammer" to Linda. (Apologies for the mixed sports metaphors but stick with me). Linda now had control over where this negotiation would go next and I was relishing the thought of watching. After adjusting her posture, not that it needed adjusting, and squaring shoulders with Charles she began the pitch that I have no doubt she had rehearsed.

"Charles, we've talked about this countless times. Sean and I are not convinced that you have a concept of the inordinate hidden costs of this project. We've tried to..." and that's where Charles lost it and breached etiquette by butting in.

"Criminy! Did you hear what we offered? Are you seriously going to throw around 'hidden costs' in an attempt to railroad us? I don't believe it! Linda, we've been over this a thousand times. We have conceded to all of your requirements around control, payments, and operations and have already agreed in principle to the price tag of each. The only thing left is finalizing your compensation. Tell me you are not going to play some 'hidden costs' card to squeeze out more money."

I couldn't tell if the incredulous tone of voice was sincere or an act but it didn't matter. What I could tell was that he immediately realized his faux pax and internally acknowledged that he had grossly underestimated his adversary. His body language made it clear that he wouldn't make that mistake again.

In a calm voice Linda picked up where she left off. "Charles, as I was saying…" (I'm certain she was inclined to reach across the table and touch his hand in a reassuring manner, like she had done with me countless times, but that would be totally improper for this context). "We have tried to tell you that as admirable as this humanitarian effort is, it is all for naught if we're not conscious of the potential collateral damage. Building bridges, sheltering the homeless, safer roads are all wonderful things but there exists a very real and plausible possibility, or more accurately stated, probability, that we will cause harm to many people unintentionally in the way of lost jobs, lost income, loss of self-esteem and a host of other unforeseeable harms that are side-effects of the process." Charles was trying to hide his contempt for her words but was doing a poor job of it.

"You are also well aware that our personal interests lean toward the humanitarian aspect of this venture as opposed to the financial aspects. So, it is with those things in mind that I propose a different figure."

Then, with the timing of a well-practiced comedian who knows exactly when and how to deliver a punch line she said "We insist on 1 percent of what you have offered. There are some conditions of course. We believe that ten million dollars represents generational wealth for us and will provide us with all we need for life.

"So, what do you think?" she concluded.

Talk about a pregnant pause. You could have heard a pin drop. The accountant perked up in his seat, the other lawyer looked baffled and the CEO didn't flinch. Charles, predictably, had been listening intently and showed no reaction other than stopping that contemptable look he had been trying to hide. He simply inquired, "Conditions?"

Boo Yah!!! She had him.

Linda and I had discussed this so often I knew exactly what her next play was. We were minutes away from closing on a win-win deal that was going to rock this planet. She smoothly reached into her briefcase and selected the contract with the gold tape. With an unnoticeable sleight of hand, she removed the tape before placing it on the table and sliding it in Charles' direction. "I'm confident that you will not find anything in there that we haven't already talked about and that you haven't already verbally agreed to in principle."

"Such as...?"

"You can read the details at your leisure but in addition to what we have already agreed to verbally, it specifies an additional $990 million to be distributed as specified: $150 million allocated to tuition grants for misplaced workers, $50 million for health departments in impacted regions, $200 million for trade schools to adjust their curriculum to be more appropriate for the 'new normal'. There's more but you get the gist. So, I ask you again, what do you think?"

Charles took a quick look around the table making eye contact with each individual on his team, ostensibly to gain consensus from each one. Everyone participated in the charade but everyone also knew we were done only when the CEO gave that slight nod of his head.

Game... Set... Match! Touchdown! Home run! Swish! Done deal!

3. THE BEGINNING OF THE MIDDLE

> *Whatever is not forbidden, is compulsory*

LENIUM IS BORN

Now that the partnership with *The Consortium* was inevitable, we kicked into gear taking out short term loans we would pay off as soon as the paperwork cleared for *The Consortium* deal. We picked up where we left off, only now we had the money and resources to seriously make headway.

Marissa fit right in contributing from day one. She was absolutely giddy with anticipation when she found out we were acquiring one of the Q-Tron quantum computers. We chose Q-Tron  because their approach utilizes quadratic unconstrained binary optimizations that outperform other approaches in regard to the pre-processing overhead associated with annealing-based approaches.

Our choice was the *Hyper 4000* that has a design that enables 40-way connectivity, utilizes over ten thousand qubits, and makes use of quantum coherence in a multilayered protocol stack that is noise tolerant, self-correcting and can scale.

All of that translates into massive computing power at our fingertips.

Over the next six months we were able to formulate a collection of deliverables that would comprise the end-to-end quantum construction process. Lee, Marissa, and I kept each other updated continuously through the day, but today we held a somewhat uncharacteristic formal "status update meeting" to bring Linda up to speed on the accomplishments so far, and to mark the momentous occasion by popping a cork. All four of us were present because this would not be exclusively about the science, it would include the practical aspects required to make the science real in the world.

"Lee, why don't you start us off and fill us in on what you've got for us," was my kickoff statement.

He took over with uncommon zeal. "Mark this day on your calendars because today is the day that marks the birth of the next element of the periodic table because today is the day that, drum roll please, Lenium is born." he announced with the satisfaction of dad seeing his newborn son for the first time, while the participants in the room exchanged congratulatory high-fives. He continued, "Lenium is special because its atomic weight and immense number of valence electrons enable it to form bonds with other elements on the order of 10^7

kilojoules per mole. These valence electrons reside in the heretofore nonexistent R period – the eighth energy level or shell of the periodic table – and due to the phase of the electrons they are disbursed across multiple suborbitals."

"Do you have any you can show us?" asked Linda innocently.

"Well, no, that's not really practical. I should mention that Lenium, being artificially fabricated has a half-life of approximately 1.8 x 10^{-5} seconds, that's eighteen microseconds. That simply means that all those valence electrons will want to normalize and the substance begins to emit alpha particles which causes the decay and it reverts to its constituent parts.

"Now in anticipation of your next question, 'Where is the value in that?', that's where the *molecular electron exciter* comes in. When we create the lenium, we use the MEE to leverage the strong forces for bonding. By capturing the emitted alpha particles, we can bond Lenium to a combination of iron, aluminum, chorine, all commonly found in nature, and produce a compound we call *Trilenium Quadra Chloride* or TQC which is stable and very malleable. It has the consistency of modeling clay but is technically, in chemistry terms, a liquid. TQC is something I can show you."

Sean abruptly jumped in with "But you would still not be impressed until you see the work Marissa has been doing with her 3-D printer. Marissa?"

"What Sean is referring to is that while all that work Lee has been doing – at enormous cost I might add – is all well and good but at the end of the day all he's really got to show for it is a rather colorless form of Play-Doh," she teased. "The real value is only realized when we mold that clay into something practical, and that we can do with a form of 3-D printing.

"The way it works is Lee's process produces the raw TQC that the printer consumes to shape the object we want while it is still in its raw form. I've been working with a commercially available industrial printer for a while now experimenting with programming required to produce some simple gardening tools. I've also shown that TQC has amazing cohesion capabilities enabling us to make fine grain objects like a hair comb. We don't know yet how fine we can go, that's not the emphasis right now.

"Since you like show-and-tell, here's some samples of stuff we've produced," and she reached down and placed a typical shovel blade and fork of a garden rake on the table. "We're limited on the size of what we make but the size of the printer we're using. I'd like to work with you on getting a partnership setup with some printer manufacturer so we can get a customized version that is more construction-friendly with the TQC process."

"One question," Lee teasingly interjected, "How useful is the printer and all your programming without any TQC to feed it?"

"That's a very valid question. Let me get back to you on that," she playfully replied.

Linda then chimed in, "But from everything you've told me, this shovel and rake should be colorless clay but they aren't, they are very hard. There must be more than you've mentioned."

Marissa bowed slightly while extending her arms across her body with palms up in my direction. I stood up and took over.

"Great segue to the final step, without which we only have molded forms of clay in elaborately shaped but useless forms." I then waited for the obligatory "ughs" from Lee and Marissa before continuing. "The final step is where we leverage the transformational qualities of the TQC that Lee has most meticulously engineered, and the artistry of the creative programming of Marissa's to transform the clay into an object with purpose." The room recognized the overworked verbiage as a shallow attempt at reconciliation.

"This is where we target the clay with just the right gamma rays thereby molecularly transforming the 'clay' from its liquid state into its solid state that has the density of heavy corrugated cardboard, the strength of steel and the oxidation qualities of aluminum."

Linda then thoughtfully asked, "So, what do you make the TQC from? You can't just create it; you have to transform it from something into something else. And the other question is where to you get the energy for those transformations? Everything has a cost. How do we make this work in a profit-oriented world?"

Sean replied, "Therein lies the beauty. We have demonstrated we can formulate TQC from theoretically any combination of elements because at the quantum level everything is made from the same quarks – fermions, leptons, protons, neutrons, electrons, etc. We just restructure the parts to our liking in a way that the natural laws of physics embraces. We will choose to use substances that are plentiful and cheap, like sand, salt, and water.

"As for the energy part, that's the area needing the most work. We have an idea that is groundbreaking and plausible, but it will take some time to fully develop. It is the key to enabling the ability to take on enormous projects like bridge building, road surfacing and skyscraper framing. The early application will have lower ROI but that will buy time to warm the world up to the concept as well and do all that social awareness stuff that you do. Over time, the tech improves, costs plummet and projects get more and more ambitious.

"In the long term, and this alludes to what Marissa was saying earlier, we integrate the four distinct steps into a single inseparable contiguous process. By that I mean that we produce the raw lenium, bond it with elements to form the TQC, mold and shape it, and solidify it all in what appears to be a single step in the timeframe a human can observe. At the quantum level, each of those steps will happen in such rapid succession that energy transfer, both in and out, can be leveraged instantaneously with no loss. That's the real key, it happens so fast it's done almost before it starts.

"Let's use road construction as one possibility. You've seen how today road construction consists of multiple steps of grading, laying sand, spreading oil, laying asphalt, and steam rolling it flat. Imagine a scenario where we just 'spray' TQC and we're done. We will be able to 'spray paint' fences into existence. The applications are endless.

"But all that will take time," I concluded.

"So, if this stuff is so indestructible, what do you do when you don't want that road anymore or you want to tear down the house framed with TQC?" asked Linda.

"Oh, I forgot to mention it will be recyclable. By immersing the solidified TQC with the complimentary alpha and beta waves with inverted wavelengths – anti-waves if you will – the substance reverts to its liquid state and the TQC can be collected and repurposed."

"Wouldn't that enable terrorists with the right equipment to destroy what we build?" Linda asked.

"Can't they do that today to conventional construction with dynamite? And dynamite is a LOT cheaper than designing and building an inverse photon transpiler. Furthermore, as of now, there are no instructions on how to do it on YouTube." I reasoned. "But seriously, are we creating any new problems here? Let's be certain we understand the risks. So far, I don't think we're making anything any worse, do you?"

"You're probably right. Let's keep thinking about it. Is that it?" Linda asked.

"Yep, that's it," Sean replied.

"Well then, I see two missing things critical to our success. First, I need to get busy with the printer folks, the social folks, the trade schools, state education departments, and let's not forget *The Consortium*. And second of all, we need to pop the cork on that bottle celebrate some of the most exceptional work this world has ever seen. You guys are freaking awesome."

LIFE IS GRAND

Disaster prevention was baked into the solution. Marissa was the one responsible for producing the threat model analysis. Borrowing from her security knowledge in computer networking, she went through a process of identifying and modeling all the threat vectors of each of the four distinct processes. Then for each vector, subjecting it to a probability analysis to determine projected probability of error. Identifying the vectors for a given interaction was typically simple, what was not simple was identifying all the possible entity interactions. This was the kind of stuff I hated to do but Marissa loved it. She derived her own error threshold limit she defined as the *Simplified Heuristic Intolerance Threshold*. This represented the maximum allowed margin of error for any given threat vector. It became evident in time the name was a bit contrived so that when I would ask, *'What's the margin of error?'* she could reply *'Smaller than S.H.I.T.'*. I was beginning to think she was spending too much time with Lee and me.

Within a couple of months, we launched our first commercial set of products. *The Consortium* had teamed up with a couple of local hardware stores in Enid

Oklahoma to run a pilot program first. Based on the favorable response we expanded to some of the national big box stores. We built a very modest manufacturing facility in a 2,500 square foot warehouse where we made shovels and rakes reflective of previous prototyping efforts. We had them placed on the shelves next to the tried-and-true name brands of *Stanley*® and *True Temper*®. Our products were priced only slightly higher than other products of comparable quality despite the fact they were selling at way below our cost to produce. Profit was not the objective, finding out if they held up to our expectations was.

The response was overwhelming, exceeding our wildest expectations. Everyone loved the weight ratio and wanted more. We decided it was time to expand but do we scale up or scale out. It was time to find out what Linda had in mind.

"So, what's the plan now, oh enlightened one? We've apparently got something here that is quite marketable. Do we build a bigger facility with a bigger photon cannon or do we build lots of smaller factories with smaller output?" I asked.

"Photon cannon? Seriously? Is that what you're calling the TQC transducer now?" she asked incredulously.

"Depends on whether I'm talking to a corporate exec or a real person. You have to admit 'photon cannon' is not only more intuitive; it's also more fun."

"Whatever. As to your question about how to scale, I'm of the opinion we scale up with the bigger photon cannon," she replied with a little too much emphasis on the last two words. By scaling up we keep things under our direct control longer; increase our production capabilities; and we get to start prototyping new larger products where our value-add proposition gets stronger. By scaling out we get only the first benefit and at much greater cost."

So that was it. We expanded into a manufacturing facility that had produced large equipment like tractors and excavators. Soon we were producing shelves, roofing products and siding. Shipping costs for these were drastically lower than other products and other manufacturers were getting concerned. That's where Linda would get involved and direct them to *The Consortium* where they could get involved. All the good things we had hoped for were happening. And predictably, all the negative things were happening also. People were feeling their jobs were being threatened, and they were right. Some were getting depressed and there were small cells of defiance. Fortunately, all these things had been anticipated and planned for. There was help for anyone who wanted it, and probably the single most important thing about it was that it was all funded without any government tax money.

Our projects were getting larger, the TQC cohesion chamber had now been integrated with, and physically into, the device that served to shape the clay (it no longer resembled a 3-D printer in any way) and with the photon cannon. We called it *Big Gus* for no reason other than it was easy to say. We never marketed what the process was, we just referred to it as our "new and innovative proprietary approach." Certain words like "fermion" or "nuclear" were forbidden because of bad connotations with the latter and nobody understood the former, and people fear what they don't understand, and they kill what they fear.

In a few years, many major universities were issuing degrees in Quantum Construction. Linda had retained the trademark but greatly reduced the barriers for using the term such that any entity could fill out some simple forms prohibiting them from profiteering and they would be granted usage rights without an exchange of any money. Inflation had stabilized and stopped. The feds hadn't changed the prime interest rate in eighteen months. The process was being used without profiting yet, but it also was paying for itself. What could have been profits were injected back into the community according to by-laws of *The Consortium*. Some local jurisdictions had even dropped or eliminated certain tax levies that were no longer needed. Charitable giving was on the rise and the entertainment industry was thriving like never before, all because people needed less money and had more time. The dream was being realized.

Not long after that the first bridge was built in Vaduz, Austria. We all traveled there together to oversee the operation. It was by far the single biggest project that had ever been attempted. Even though the technology was now advanced enough to add some artistic flair, the designers opted to use QC for just the fundamentals and allow the local craftsmen the opportunity to dress it up. They even added remarkably exquisite web of cables that was entirely for esthetics. The cables served no functional or structural purpose but they were magnificent to look at.

THE HICCUP

Right near the end of the first (and only) week, as the construction was completing, an anomaly occurred. The last row of bridge pilons physically grew by 0.5 cm. Lee was very troubled by it. Marissa and I weren't so troubled as we were curious. This was imperceptible to the human eye, well within the tolerances for traditional construction, and in and of itself nothing to be alarmed about. We felt it could be easily explained though we had no plausible explanation. Everyone did agree that it was an anomaly and that we needed to know why it happened. A team of divers was deployed to go down and sample the base soil and take all kinds of temperature readings, soil samples and water samples. We reached out to local seismic measuring stations to obtain records of any seismic activity in the area regardless of how small. Marissa, of course had ample computer audit logs that captured in minute detail every single event of the construction. Additionally, as part of the process a computerized laser tape measure actively recorded all progress at a distance in real-time in increments of 0.1 seconds and an accuracy to within 0.1 millimeters. Before we left, we remeasured every expanse of the bridge.

A slew of standard stability tests were performed and the results far exceeded anything that had ever been accomplished using conventional construction techniques. We felt assured that the bridge was in fact stable and we headed back home to analyze the data.

After a day and night of jet-lag recovery we all got together to debrief. Marissa had already been pouring over the voluminous amount of data we had so she started the conversation."

"I've been comparing the laser tape's measurements of both during and after construction to that comparable data in the computer audit logs and they don't agree. When Big Gus formed that last foot of bridge, the full width of 52.353 meters was completed. That measurement is confirmed by the real-time laser tape. Only later, something occurred that caused the fully set TQC to grow 0.5 cm. And you know, that's simply not possible."

Silence filled the room.

"Any thoughts?" I asked. Lee started first.

"I'm with Marissa, that's impossible. Every projection we've ever made in hundreds of thousands of simulations has demonstrated repeatedly that the only way, er, the only known way that could happen is if the nuclear bonding continued by some means and started consuming mass outside of the scope of the photon cannon. And that's beyond comprehension."

"But what's the one thing we know is different about this run than any other to date?" Marissa responded directly to Lee.

"Scale. This is the first very large scale run we've ever attempted. Do you think there's are relationship there somewhere?" he responded.

"Yes, I do," was her reluctant reply.

"How so?" he replied just as Linda was entering the room.

"Hey, what's up everyone?" Linda mentioned cheerily only to be met with Sean's upheld hand to politely shush her in a way that informed her she'd just walked in on something significant.

"Marissa, continue. How so?" asked Sean.

"Well, I can't prove any of what I'm going to say but I do feel very strongly down to core of my bones that this is all related in some way to Korkov's principle of nuclear cohesion at large scale."

"Oh, for crying out loud! Korkov? Seriously?" shouted Sean.

"Now wait, before you dismiss me let me speak. I know you don't like the man and I know his theory is as of yet unproven. But that does not necessarily mean it is wrong. I'm just asking the question, regardless of how remote, what if it is correct? If so, it could possibly explain some things."

"Like what?"

"Like, if the strong forces of nuclear cohesion do in fact tend to alternate amplitudes under situations of large scale and therefore shift to weak forces, then TQC could, possibly, suffer from the same effect – at large scale."

"And like I always have said," Sean retorted a little calmer now, "that's a very intriguing theory but where's the proof? Without proof it's just a fairy tale."

"I disagree," countered Marissa. "Without proof it is just unproven but potentially no less true. For example, before Einstein came along time warps were considered a fairy tale. No one could prove it was real. There *was* no proof. But special relativity changed that. We now recognize time dilation is real but it was real all the time, just unproven."

Again, there was a hush in the room. The next steps would be determined by Sean's reaction.

"Sean," said Lee gently, "You know we have to look into what she said, right?"

"Yeah, I know. What do you have in mind?"

Marissa boldly then stated, "We have to go talk to him."

"I'll think about it." Sean said quietly. "In the meantime, let's keep analyzing the data we have. There's got to be another explanation."

THE VISIT

That night Linda and I were revisiting the day's events in the comfort of our living room. I was doing the revisiting and Linda was doing the listening. She knew I liked to think out loud because the act of verbalizing helped me see things I otherwise would look past. This happened countless times when I would be writing some computer software and hit a roadblock. I would explain the problem to her in excruciating detail all the while listening to myself simultaneously to validate that what I was saying made sense, often times backing up to restate something that was incomplete or unclear. It was astonishing how many times the process ended with "That's it! That's the problem!" And all she had to do was keep reading her book and nod occasionally.

It was like that tonight, only tonight I was arguing with myself.

"You know Korkov is a quack, right? That isn't something new."

"Oh, sure he's got book learning and admittedly knows something about quantum physics, but that doesn't change the fact that he's a quack and an idiot."

"And the unscrupulous S.O.B. has no moral compass, no ethical north star."

"But that doesn't change the fact that I've got a problem that can't be explained away. Yet, that is. We'll figure it out. We couldn't have gotten this far if QC was so fundamentally flawed."

"Then again, if that's true, then why am I stressing so much?"

Breaking out of my self-induced tranced I looked over to Linda and asked, "Do you have anything to offer?"

"Today is Wednesday, how does Monday sound?" she replied.

"For what?"

"For a meeting with Korkov. I'm pretty sure I can get the arrangements made to meet along with the airline tickets and hotel. Marissa will need to be there too."

With a tone of resignation I replied, "That was pretty presumptuous of you. Let's assume I say yes, and that's a huge assumption, what makes you think he'd ever consider meeting with me? He's seen my criticism of his work."

Linda replied, "Oh, he'll see you. His personal assistant is working on getting Monday completely blocked out for time with you. How do you feel about going one-on-one with him for an entire day?"

"Bring it on, I say. Can you get him to block a week? I'm pretty sure that's how long my opening statements will take."

"I'll see what I can do" was her sarcastic and appeasing reply. I knew full well I had just been played and goaded into a meeting I would never have thought I'd agree to.

We had a flight of about fourteen hours to get to Prague. That seemed like a supreme waste of time for a two-hour meeting, but Linda insisted we meet face-to-face. Linda booked first-class seats because she knew the less stressed I was from traveling, the greater the chances the meeting would be productive. The plane was configured such that we were able to turn the seats of one row around and the three of us could face each other and plan strategy. We were fortunate to find the extra seat was unoccupied. I said "plan strategy" but what I really meant was "go over the ground rules". I knew Marissa was enamored with Korkov and I needed to impress on her that under no circumstances were any of us to share any specific details regarding QC. We needed to stay abstract and divulge nothing about QC and especially not about our problem. Simultaneously, we needed to extract all that secret information I was convinced he was hiding about his research. *'I don't know, maybe we can actually learn something interesting,'* I thought to myself. I vowed to give it my best shot but made no promises.

We finished the planning session, had a couple of drinks and a remarkably satisfying dinner for airline food, and then I got about six hours of restful sleep. I always slept well on airplanes. The dull monotonous hum of the engines always blocked out all distractions and I slept like a baby.

When we arrived, we got a taxi to the hotel and got settled in. It was going to be a quick trip so I never unpacked I just worked from the suitcase, as did Linda. Before we went to bed, we went downstairs to the piano bar and a woman was at the black grand piano playing a series of classic jazz tunes. Music always seems to transcend language. We each had a glass of wine then retired to get rested for the big day tomorrow.

In the morning we had breakfast together then shuttled off to meet at Korkov's home. It was a surprisingly modest structure in what appeared to be to be middle class neighborhood, but what did I know about the Czech Republic. We were met at the door by a smartly dressed woman who took us through the impeccably decorated home to an unusually large office or den or something that doesn't have an American description. But it was large. Once there, the woman left prior to introductions leaving me to wonder if she was his wife or his domestic help. I caught myself and thought, '*Stay focused.*'

Korkov introduced himself and looked at Linda saying, "And you must be the Dr. Linda Blake that Marcella coordinated with to arrange this meeting. I'm very pleased to meet you."

He then turned to me and extending his right hand he said, "You must be the venerable Dr. Sean Blake. I am honored. I have hoped for this day for years and today that hope is fulfilled."

"The honor is mine Dr. Korkov." I managed to say while I grasped his hand with mine and applied firm pressure until he released first. I was proud of myself for the effort.

Turning to Marissa he said, "And who are you my charming guest?" while also kissing her hand.

"My name is Marissa Faraday and I work with Sean and Linda."

"Excellent. Shall we sit? Now, please, to what do I owe this special gathering?" I had to say one thing, his English was impeccable and his manners well practiced. Ok, that's two things but who's counting.

"Dr. Korkov, we're here because we're interested in gaining a bit more insight into your work with nuclear cohesion. I've always been fascinated by..." I began before he cut me off.

"Dear Dr. Blake. Do you take me for a fool?" he butted in. Before I could say "Yes", I felt a sharp pinch under the table on my thigh from Linda who sitting next to me. Korkov continued, "Please forgive the interruption but let's drop the pretense. I've read your criticisms of my work and you are not fascinated with anything I'm doing. I'm also aware of your work in Quantum Construction. So, shall we just get to the elephant in the living room so to speak and start talking about the problem you experienced in Vaduz? You are wondering if my 'fairy tale theory' might possibly explain the anomalies you experienced, yes?"

I thought, *'Oh crap, he knows way more than I expected.'*

Marissa jumped in having seen where the conversation was going and attempted to smooth over years of animosity in just a few sentences. An admirable but futile cause. "Dr. Korkov, I too have been following your work for years now and let me just say that Dr. Blake and I are not fully aligned in our views. I'd like to know more about what prompted you to explore nuclear cohesion as it relates to mass. You've defined the constant for force depletion theorizing that any atomic mass that exceeds that threshold reverts to weak force bonding in proportion to the delta. What observations and/or speculation of yours convinced you that a threshold like this actually exists?"

He replied, "It is not a matter of observation; it is a matter of deductive reasoning. Nearly everything in this universe has effective limits. Massless particles, photons for example, travel at the 186,000 miles per second but can never exceed that. A black hole possesses gravity so forceful nothing can escape it but only up to the event horizon, after which the black hole's pull is less than escape velocity. Objects falling to earth accelerate at thirty-two feet per second per second but only until they reach terminal velocity. With all these visible patterns, how could one think that there is *not* a threshold for strong nuclear force, the strongest of the four forces in the universe?"

"I see," said Marissa, "What then has been the biggest hurdle for you in validating the *Korkov Constant*?"

"The biggest hurdle is being able to prove to the science world of the threshold via observation. In today's world the amount of nuclear mass required to reach the threshold has never been fabricated and it does not exist in nature. I do suspect that you, Dr. Blake, with your quantum construction have achieved what I have not been able to. But that is only suspicion on my part. I believe that if you would share the details of what you are doing with me, we could work together for the benefit of us both: I would get my theory validated; you would explain the anomaly you have in QC. Is that something you would consider?"

Anticipating what my response would be, Linda jumped in with a more politically and socially palatable response, "Dr. Korkov, it is not quite as easy as that. We are engaged contractually with numerous entities worldwide and there are limits as to how much we can share without consensual agreement by all affected parties. That is not to say it can't be done, but it is to say that Sean himself cannot make that call."

It was now my turn to make a sincere attempt at compromise. "So, just for argument's sake let's say we can get approval from *The Consortium* to work with you. That will take time, Linda would be best at estimating how much. Since you have no contractual constraints, would you in the interim be willing to share with me your private calculations and other work that has failed to prove your constant? That could be useful to me and opens the possibility that I could discover the missing element you need to complete your work. Even without *The Consortium* approval there would be no ethical or contractual breach because your work is not related to mine at all, and even if it is, it is a tangential relation at best."

"Dr. Blake, you already have full knowledge of my work. I, on the other hand, have no real knowledge of yours. Until we can have mutual trust and total disclosure, I don't see how we can work together. I suggest you contact this consortium that you speak of and do the needful. Until then, it is apparent we both must protect our respective intellectual property. Do you not agree?"

"I'm not certain I agree, but I do now, understand your position quite clearly. Linda, is there anything else to cover?" I asked with a tone of finality.

"I've got one last question Dr. Korkov if I could," blurted Marissa.

"Please..." he acknowledged.

"If I understand your formula for the *Korkov Constant* correctly, your calculations are centered exclusively around nuclear mass. Isn't it logical that atomic density would play some role in the diminished strong force?"

Korkov replied, "An interesting concept to be sure but as you know, density would be a product of both mass and space. Atomically, it is electromagnetism that constrains the electrons to their assigned orbitals and the size of the orbitals is what ultimately determines occupied space and therefore density. So, I don't see any plausible relationship between the two."

"Thank you," Marissa politely replied.

Linda took over, "Dr. Korkov, thank you for taking time out of your busy day for us. I hope we can keep channels of communication open through these coming months. I will approach *The Consortium* as to the viability of us building a working relationship we both can accept."

With that, we took our leave and went back to the hotel.

In the cab while returning to the hotel Linda broke the silence, "Sean, I was proud of how you handled yourself today."

"Really, the welt on my thigh would indicate otherwise. I thought you would be mad at me for not compromising." I grumpily replied.

"No. You just said what you needed to say. It was all truthful and appropriate. He made it clear he has firm convictions for sharing information. By the way, you know *The Consortium* is not a roadblock here. Getting approval from them is a no-brainer, but we do need to jump through that hoop first. As for today, it is way too early to release our data in an uncontrolled fashion to the world at large.

"You may not think so but this whole trip for a face-to-face visit was very helpful to me to understand the man," she continued. "Body language doesn't come across over the phone or virtual meetings. Besides, this subject is not dead just delayed. You keep working on what you do and let me take this from here, agreed?"

I replied gratefully, "Agreed. And thanks for not ragging on me."

A little later Marissa turned to me and asked, "Sean, I'm curious, if you were Korkov and convinced you were on to something big, would you take any stock in my final question to Korkov regarding considering atomic density as part of the computations for the *Blake Constant*?"

I chuckled at her transparent attempt at enlisting me as the owner of the concept by the use of the new name.

I thought it was cute enough to warrant and honest and thoughtful response. "I suppose, if it was my theory, which is not, I would feel obligated to investigate any concept that could be potentially helpful. But more than that, I do think your idea is a good one that deserves a chance to be proven wrong before being dismissed as simply not having 'any plausible relationship'."

"Thanks. Your opinion means a lot to me."

Soon we were pulling up to the hotel to grab lunch, gather our things, and head to the airport for a very long flight home.

4. THE END OF EVERYTHING

> *When the preferable is not available,*
> *the available becomes preferable.*

THE CALCULATED RISK

We continued our work with Big Gus while Linda kept working with *The Consortium* and fixing other outside issues. We were making progress every day. There had been enough time now for us to review all of the data from the Vaduz bridge run and other than confirming there was an anomaly, we knew little more as to the cause. The smoking gun continued to be that some behavior was changing slightly once mass reached some threshold. We had identified that theoretical threshold at which it apparently happened in Vaduz but could not confirm the behavior change without experimentation and observation. And observation would require a big project.

There was a new potential project coming our way that would be slightly larger than Vaduz in regard to material volume. It was in Switzerland where a rainwater reclamation project was planning to build a series of cistern-like repositories for capturing rainwater from snow melting in the Alps. Discussions were currently happening between the old-school traditionalists that wanted to construct using traditional methods and the usually younger progressives that were excited about QC. It was the usual discussion of tried-and-true vs. new-and-unproven, risk vs. reward. Linda was included in some of those discussions and she disclosed everything. We had no desire to sell anyone on our technology, in fact, in this case we fully disclosed the Vaduz anomaly and what we knew and what we didn't know. Total transparency. In a rather unexpected twist, we noticed that served to bolster trust rather than erode it.

Internally, Lee, Marissa, and I continued to assess the risk associated with doing another big "run" (as we called it) without knowing all the answers.

"The question we need to answer now is whether it is responsible for us to do another large run before we know more about the cause, or can we cautiously do a run to capture more information to determine the cause," I threw out to the others as we gathered in the conference room.

Marissa reported, "Given that the one differentiating factor appears to be mass, I've added telemetry to Big Gus's diagnostics reporting subsystem to capture in greater detail the transitions of the four quantum numbers: energy, angular momentum, magnetic orientation, and electron phase or spin. If the problem is in fact related to the existence of the *Korkov Constant* I'm certain the new data will give us what we need to identify and solve it."

"But what are the chances that acquiring the data ends up creating some process that gets out of control? We just don't really know what is possible." countered Lee.

Marissa countered, "Don't you think that if we are cautious and once the run gets to the threshold we've identified, that we can throttle Big Gus down to a crawl while we observe and learn. At the first sign of trouble, we stop. I'm sure we could design the run in a layered approach such that if we had to stop, they could complete the project with traditional techniques on top of what we had done. They would get a lot of value from QC and we would get some answers."

The discussion continued for hours like this with each of us contributing what we felt was additional telemetry to be added. Finally, Lee decided that we had discussed all there was to discuss.

"So, Sean, that's it. That's all there is. Unfortunately, you have to make a call with limited data. I for one am glad I'm not you today. It sucks to be the boss sometimes."

"Yeah, it sucks to be me today," I confirmed reluctantly before changing tones to exude confidence. "So, here's what we're going to do. We're going to go forward... *cautiously*, and with full disclosure. We hide nothing and we stop at the first, even insignificant sign of trouble. We may have dodged the bullet in Vaduz, or maybe we could have continued to a bridge twice that size with a margin of error that most would deem immeasurable. What I do know is that by shutting down QC for large runs we'll never know the truth."

Marissa added, "I concur, Sean. I think that's the right approach. That's what I'd do."

"Same here." Lee added.

Sean appended one last comment, "I'll run it by Linda when she gets home tonight. Until then, keep thinking. We need answers."

Marissa immediately went to adding the new diagnostics to Big Gus.

One week to the day later we were getting everything setup to begin with the Swiss project. We had gone over all the possible points at which we might shut down with the Swiss project planners. Everyone was convinced that even if we had to shut down, completing the project through other means would still be financially beneficial and faster. Linda had agreed to the approach with the single caveat that regardless of the outcome, whether we shut down or don't, and regardless of whether or not we got all the data we needed, we would never do a third large run until we had answers. Everyone, even Marissa, welcomed that constraint.

The Trilux Adapter

We started the project on schedule three days later. In addition to Big Gus, we also had at our ready the inverse photon transpiler which we called Little Debbie for no real reason other than Big Gus was masculine so this should be feminine. Little Debbie was the tool that was capable of reversing the process and 'melting' the hardened TQC back into the liquid TQC that was clay-like and stable. That was there just in case. Marissa had added two additional monitors to Big Gus enabling us to watch in real time the graphs of the four quantum numbers as well as animated simulations of data samples representing the nuclear cohesion. She had demoed this new telemetry back in the lab and it was exciting to actually watch what was going on underneath all that chemistry and science.

The moment had come and preparation was complete. We were as ready as we would ever be. Big Gus was fired up and the construction began. As anticipated, everything went like it always had gone the tens of thousands of times we had done this before. Over the next few days, the operation went flawlessly and we were even blessed with great weather for the Alps. We had projected we wouldn't reach the determining threshold until the fourth day. Today was the fourth day.

The nearer we got to the threshold the more we throttled back Big Gus. This not only improved our ability to react quicker but had the benefit of more detailed diagnostics at far more granular recording intervals. As soon as we hit the threshold, we stopped Big Gus and monitored the diagnostic telemetry. Everything flatlined. So far so good. We started Big Gus up again to continue at a pace that was imperceptible to the human eye. The people watching the process from the guarded and segregated spectator section thought we had stopped. We knew billions of particle collisions and energy transformations were happening at incomprehensible speeds, even though you couldn't' see them.

"Hold on a sec..." Marissa uttered.

"SHUT IT DOWN!" I yelled in reaction which was completely unnecessary since Lee had already stopped Big Gus.

"What? What are you looking at?" I asked.

"It's happening. Right now, it's happening," she answered.

"What? What's happening?" I repeated.

"Look... Look at these two numbers. Here is the mass that Big Gus generated," she said pointing to a green dotted line on the graph. It was a line that had been incrementally climbing until Big Gus was shut down at which point it flatlined. "And here's the mass as is being measured in real-time by our diagnostics module."

"You're right, it's happening. Fascinating. That is absolutely fascinating." I echoed in a tone that could only be described as a whisper as we all watched the second line continue to creep ever so slowly up.

Lee then quietly asked, "What do we do now?" After waiting for and not receiving an answer he added, "Boss?"

With both of them looking for direction I whispered to them, "Don't freak out. Follow my lead." I felt they still needed something a bit more substantial so I added, "I've got this."

Then I stood up and with all the acting skills I could muster I yelled as loud as I could, "Damnit to hell! Why now? Why is it always at the worst possible moment?" The other two were befuddled but both played it nicely by each grabbing their forehead and dropping and shaking their head in disappointment.

As I had hoped, Romain, the on-site coordinator and PR man, hastily made his way to the console.

In an accent I couldn't identify he said, "What is it Dr. Blake? Is there a problem?"

"Yeah, there's a problem. Ooh, that's frustrating." I exclaimed. "Lee, do you want to explain it to Romain?"

"Uh... certainly Dr. I just need to check one more thing," he replied hesitantly while giving me a quizzical look mixed in with an icy stare letting me know he didn't like being the subject of my shenanigans.

I took over again, "Well, I don't need to check anything. I've seen this before. The trilux adapter on the motherboard has fried. We can't do anything more until we replace it."

Marissa and Lee looked at each other and silently moved their lips as if to say, "Trilux adapter?"

Marissa was first to catch on. She pushed Lee lightly on the shoulder and forcing back her smile said, "Yeah, the trilux adapter fried. I knew that."

"Well how long will it take to replace it?" Romain justifiably asked.

I looked quizzically back at Lee to let him know I was having fun and he wasn't off the hook yet. "I *know* it's a trilux adapter that fried," he emphatically stated first in order to defend his honor then added, "But repair time depends on *which* trilux adapter blew – the high voltage one that takes a very *long* time, or the low voltage one that is quickly replaced." Then he quickly added, "And Dr. Blake is the only one who can determine that."

I winked at Lee as if to say, "Well played," then turned to Romain, "Romain my friend, this is going to take some time, at the very least the rest of the day. We've got all the parts we need in our truck but we'll need to fix, and test, all that complicated computer stuff. Why don't you send everyone home for today and we'll pick back up tomorrow? I'll call you later tonight to confirm. It will probably be late. OK?"

With that, he nodded and released the rest of the crew then sent all the spectators home. We were free to get back to analyzing the problem without distractions.

I Was Right

We all gazed at the monitors and asked questions of each other. Marissa sat at the console and would replay certain animations when requested and explain the different lines on the graphs. Sometimes the labels led Lee and me to misinterpret their meaning. She was always gracious with the explanations and sometimes apologetic for choosing poorly for the label. I kept looking at my watch. It was only 11:30 AM and I knew Linda would be here soon. She wanted to be here for the whole thing but got pulled away at the last minute due to some sort of crap I didn't ask her about other than to ask when she could make it.

Marissa suddenly piped up, "Hey, look at this, guys. Look at these four lines." The screen we were looking at was immediately reset and all but four of the graph lines disappeared. "This is the same one you've been watching, the current mass. This one is the target threshold." It was a perfectly horizontal straight solid line. "This wavey line is the ratio of the valence electron amplitude over density and the other wavy line is the ratio of the valence electron amplitude over mass." There was a short pause before she added, "The time scale of the graph is from fifteen minutes prior to hitting the threshold until now."

She waited a while to let us absorb it before asking, "Do you see what I see?"

"Yes, I do. Look how the mass and density waveforms are in perfect alignment right up to the threshold line. At that point they start to shift in phase, one stretching, one compressing. It's not much but you can clearly see it." I remarked.

"Do you think it means anything? I think this could be big," Marissa asked.

"What it means," I said as I leaned over and kissed Marissa on the top of her head, "is that we have found the missing link! This is exactly what we could not find before, and we owe it all to you."

"I knew it! I was right! I knew I was right!" Marissa beamed proudly while Lee looked at me slightly puzzled. Then, after that sunk in a bit she taunted, "Do you know what else this means?"

"It also means you were right all along. There *is* a relationship between density and mass at massive scale. An incredibly intuitive conviction and brilliantly proven through verifiable scientific methods," I said in a congratulating tone.

"And...?" she egged me on.

"Do I have to?"

"And...?" she said again ever more emphatically.

"And... Vladimir Korkov is right too." I said in an almost inaudible tone. "MAYBE." I added as an emphatic afterthought.

She then tortured me with, "You mean 'probably' not 'maybe', don't you?"

"Yes. Probably." I conceded. "But do you know what the sad part is? The sad part is that we should have seen this early on, way before Vaduz. If I had just listened to you, Marissa, we would have put some time into figuring this out and would have prevented this mess. So, you just keep telling me what you think and feel." I felt like

Captain Kirk must have felt when he admonished Lieutenant Saavik to keep quoting Starfleet regulations after he had nearly destroyed the Enterprise due to his dismissal of her earlier warnings.

Changing the subject I announced, "Now, let's get back to the business at hand. It's too early to get too congratulatory. We still have a giant cistern growing and we need to stunt its growth. Lee, get on Little Debbie and let's erase the last ten minutes of the run. That shouldn't take long since Big Gus was operating so slowly. Marissa, you keep monitoring the current mass and once the mass is well below the threshold, as in at least one metric ton, we can stop."

"Okie-dokie sir!" said one.

"Roger that!" replied the other.

It was getting close to 1:00 PM, Lee was undoing our work and Marissa was watching the monitors when Linda arrived. Everyone got excited to see her when she pulled in and stopped what they were doing to rush over and share the news. I was glad to see it because we had spent weeks toiling over a problem that until this moment had appeared unsolvable. A little celebration was certainly in order.

I let them bombard Linda with all the good news for a while then eventually broke it up. "All right, let's get back to work. Once everything is stable, we can head back to the lodge and talk about how we fix Big Gus. We'll lose some time on this project for sure but once fixed we'll be able to complete it all the way so no one will care."

With that I turned my attention to Linda, "So, how was your morning?" I asked facetiously.

"Well, nothing to compare to yours, apparently. What's this I hear about Marissa being right and Korkov being right?" she countered.

"Go ahead, rub it in, rub it in. I honestly don't care because I'm really happy right now. A great weight has been lifted. We still have work to do to get things fixed and tested but now we have direction and data. The rest is easy."

"So, where are we at with the Swiss folks? I'll need to do damage control. What have you told them?"

"I told them the truth. I told them we just needed to fix the trilux adapter."

"That's not a real thing, is it? You lied to them," she replied in semi-mock disgust.

"I didn't lie, I just used a simple word they could understand.   I could have told him we need to 'recalibrate the compensation component responsible for the convergence of out-of-phase mass to density waveform ratios as impacted by electron phase shifts in atomic suborbitals,' but that wouldn't have told him anything. So, I used trilux adapter. It's an industry standard term you know. Two for five bucks at Radio Shack. Ask Lee, or Marissa, they'll vouch for me. Besides, if he didn't know what it meant he could have asked, I would have explained it," I said with a slight grin.

She acquiesced. "Now you're bullshitting me. But that's OK, no harm no foul. I can work with that. So, what's the current plan?"

I proceeded to explain what Lee and Marissa were doing and that we were planning on heading back to the lodge to get more detailed in our analysis. "Oh, by the way, you need to call Romain tonight and explain things. He is somehow under the impression that we'll be starting back up tomorrow though I don't have any idea how he could have gotten that from anything I said. You're good at these things. You can handle it. You should push things back at least a week, more if you can. You can emphasize that things are more under control now (we think) than they were when we started. And that's the honest truth."

"I'm sure it is, hon. Thanks for the tips."

Linda and I finished our conversation just about the same time Lee and Marissa finished their tasks. Marissa called over to me and asked, "We're done. Do you want to have a look?"

"Coming." I replied, gave Linda a quick kiss on the forehead and headed over.

Lee started with, "I shaved three metric tons under the threshold just to be sure. We can put them back easily once Big Gus is fixed."

Marissa followed, "And here's the look at the current mass line we were watching grow earlier. See? Flatlined, just the way we like it."

"And you're sure the monitor is still sampling the mass properly?" I challenged.

"Absolutely certain," she replied while pointing out an integer on the screen that was incrementing at a consistent and regular rate.

"All right then. Let's head back to the lodge and figure some stuff out. Great work you guys."

Disaster Happens

Back at the lodge we went over the massive amount of data that we had collected from the run. We came across what we considered to be a fortunate discovery, which was that the waveform amplitudes of the mass and density trajectories didn't change, only the frequency changed. Therefore, all we needed to do was adjust the rate of oxidation to get the waveforms to superposition with each other. The resultant constructive interference would cancel the phase shift just as it had prior to reaching the mass threshold. This was analogous to the concept used in noise cancelling headphones where the ambient background noise gets split into two signals then one signal is phase inverted. When joined back together, superpositioned so to speak, peaks of the first signal align with the valleys of the other, and valleys of the first align with the peaks of the other resulting in a flat line, meaning silence. Lee volunteered to make the trivial adjustment to the bonding gate control on Big Gus.

Once we were satisfied with our analysis, we headed back up to the construction site. Lee needed to grab some tools from the truck then head back to the lab to get the changes ready for upload to Big Gus. At the lab he could test the changes using a computerized Big Gus emulator he called Little Gus. Marissa provided him the software library with the new diagnostics he would need to certify the changes.

When we got there, Marissa immediately went to the console to start looking at the telemetry that had been captured overnight. Linda and I were surveying the construction. Everything looked just like we had left it. Marissa shouted to us, "The telemetry looks good. I don't see any changes since last night." That was an excellent sign. Linda and I continued to plot next steps to be taken with the construction.

I started explaining my thoughts to Linda, "Once Lee gets his work done, we will come back and repeat the exact same steps. We'll stop at the same point and measure everything exactly the same way we did it the first time. Exactly the same. The results should be quite different. I would like to get to the point where we stopped the first time then wait a day and check the telemetry from overnight again. If everything looks good, we go incrementally farther and wait overnight. I'd like to do this for a full week out of an overabundance of caution. Do you think you can keep the spectators away from here for a week? There won't be that much to see."

"Sure. That won't be a problem. I'll just let them know there's been a run on trilux adapters down at Radio Shack that's slowing us down," she said with a wink.

"Uh, Sean? Sean, I need you to come here. I think I made a mistake, a big one," we heard from Marissa. Linda and I headed over immediately. She continued, "I told you the telemetry looks good but that was before I adjusted the graphic display to a finer level of precision. Last night we looked at the data using four digits of precision meaning one ten thousandth of a gram of mass. It occurred to me this morning that there was possible rounding going on so I changed it to use the full seven digits of precision with which the data was captured. Looking now at the very same data only without the rounding, the cistern kept growing all night. It is barely perceptible but definitely growing. I'm so sorry. That's such a rookie mistake. I feel so stupid."

About then we heard Lee shout from a distance away, "I'm heading out now to go back to the lab. It shouldn't take too long; about four or five hours I'd guess. Call me if you need me. I've got my cellphone."

"Hold on a second Lee. Come over here. We've got a little hitch in our git-along." I shouted back.

Marissa continued, "The good news, if you need some, is that I can confirm that the everything was stable for the first four days. Not a single blip. It is only after we reached the threshold that the problem begins. It's acting like we started a chain reaction that is oh so slowly expanding."

I speculated, "What if we erase some more? We're what, three metric tons below threshold now? Let's go one hundred under and see if that stops it."

"We can try," she replied.

About that time Lee got to us and asked, "So, what's up?"

"We need to break out Little Debbie and erase some more of the cistern. This time, take it down to at least one hundred, make that three hundred metric tons below threshold." I instructed.

"Ok, but why?"

Marissa in frustration blurted, "Because I screwed up! I caused this mess."

I turned to Marissa to calm her down, "Marissa, you didn't cause anything.   Nothing you did changes anything other than delaying the discovery for what, thirty minutes or so? So don't beat yourself up. Without you, we wouldn't be this far. So, let's get focused on what our next steps need to be." After that I turned to Lee and explained the situation and then he fired up Little Debbie and went to work.

It took a bit longer to erase this time around but eventually we got there and we all stood around the console eagerly watching the graphs. It was 1:33 PM. "I don't see anything changing anymore," observed Lee. "Even the *mass growth rate* variable is stable at zero. Do you think that worked?"

"Maybe," said Marissa, "but it is also possible that we just slowed it down to a rate that our instrumentation is just not sensitive enough to detect. We're going to have to wait a day, maybe two to see for sure."

"That sounds reasonable." I agreed. "Can you setup an alert on the mass growth rate and total mass variables to notify us if or when either one of them changes?"

"Yep. That's easy to do," she acknowledged.

"Good, let's do that and head back to the lodge and see if we can make some sense out this."

I'm Scared

Back at the lodge we continued pouring over all the data we did the night before, only this time with greater precision and with the knowledge that the growth rate, albeit retarded, was still growing. We shared speculations as to what was happening and eliminated the impossible. It started getting late and without any real conclusions we decided to get some sleep and see what the telemetry would show us tomorrow. Hopefully, nothing new and we could continue brainstorming.

It was 5:12 AM when alerts started popping on everyone's cell phone. Both the mass growth rate and total mass metrics had changed and triggered alerts to each of us. We all grabbed our bathrobes and met in the hallway.

Before anyone could ask what we were going to do I said, "We can't wait any longer. We've got to take it all down. All of it."

"Isn't that a bit over-reacting and overkill?" asked Lee.

I replied sharply, "I don't see it as over-reacting and I don't care if it is overkill. This has got to stop and stop now. Have you ever thought about what happens if we can't or don't stop it? I don't even want to go there. From now on we approach this problem from a worst-case scenario perspective. I'd much rather waste this next week trying to solve a problem that doesn't need solving than move forward assuming we fixed the problem and find out we're wrong. That means there is nothing that can't be suggested. Any idea, regardless of how absurd or impossible it might sound needs to come out. No stone left unturned so to say. OK?"

I looked around for consensus from everyone which I got, each in his or her own way before I continued.

"Let's head up there and get Little Debbie going again. Linda, I need Lee here with Marissa and me to help with our analysis. Can you get someone from the project team to learn from Lee how to run Little Debbie so he is free to be with us."

"It's really pretty simple. Anyone could do it," Lee added.

Linda acknowledged, "Sure. The sun will be up soon and I'll start making some phone calls."

"Ok then. Let's get out of the hall and get dressed and have breakfast. Looks like this might be a long day." I said finalizing the discussion.

So that's what we did, with bellies full and pants on we headed up to the site.

When we arrived, there was already a couple of men there waiting for us. They were the recruits Linda had arranged for to run Little Debbie. It turns out they were both really excited to run the machine. They would have preferred to run Big Gus but they snatched at the chance to run Little Debbie. Lee got started running it and training them on the best techniques.

Marissa went to work making some changes so that her real-time telemetry would automatically upload to one of our central servers in the cloud. Additionally, she hooked up two different desk-cams so that in addition to the telemetry, we could also watch the progress remotely. We no longer needed to be present on site.

I went about gathering samples of the melted TQC that was a byproduct of Little Debbie. I wanted to analyze how it was behaving and determine if it exhibited the same growth anomaly as the 'fully cooked' TQC.

Once everyone had finished their assignments, we returned to the lab to collaborate on first determining the cause and then, hopefully, a solution. I had a theory I wanted to checkout. The law of conservation of mass assures us that since the TQC is growing in mass, the growth is coming from something else. If TQC is growing, something else is shrinking. If we knew what was being consumed it would go a long way to explaining things.

We ran a series of experiments with the clay-like TQC I brought back placing one gram in a sealed container that we filled with all varieties of gases and solids then put it under immense pressure to hopefully accelerate that growth process. We tried the gasses first, one at a time: hydrogen, helium, fluorine, neon, oxygen. No growth detected. We then tried liquids. We tried bromine, the only natural element that is liquid at room temperature, before we moved on to every other liquid we could find, with water being the obvious first choice, followed by crazy stuff like gasoline, milk, salad dressing, everything. Nothing. Nadda. Then we tested my hypothesis. We put both hydrogen and oxygen in the pressurized container and sure enough, just one gram of the liquid TQC gained mass when subjected to high pressure of those two elements. Hydrogen alone didn't do it, neither did oxygen alone, but together in gaseous form, not water, it did. With this startling discovery we came to a mutual consensus on the hypothesis as to the cause and deemed it was time to bring Linda in on the discussion.

I called Linda into the room and said, "We think we have an idea of what is going on. We're pretty confident that the molecular bonding process of the TQC has mutated into a self-generating assimilation of oxygen and hydrogen atoms and that is how the mass of TQC keeps growing."

"Do you mean the stuff is feeding and growing on water?" she asked incredulously.

I replied, "That's not technically correct but it is a fair analogy. What that means to us right now is fixing Big

Gus is not important anymore. The only thing that matters is figuring out how to stop the growth."

"And what if we can't stop the growth?" she asked nervously.

"You don't want to go there." I replied trying to dodge the question.

"I need to know. I need to hear you say it. I'm getting scared now," she pleaded.

Solemnly I explained, "If we can't stop it, it will continue to consume the available hydrogen and oxygen growing larger and larger. As it grows, its appetite will grow commensurately. We're in the snow-covered Alps where hydrogen and oxygen are released constantly as snow transitions from solid to liquid and eventually gaseous states. 'Food' will be essentially unlimited."

"So, what about thresholds, like Korkov talked about, terminal velocity and speed of light. At what point does it quit? There's always a termination threshold, right?" she pressed even more scared than before.

"That termination point will come when either all the hydrogen and oxygen on earth has been consumed or when solidified TQC covers the entire planet. Either way we're talking about total planetary annihilation."

"Sean, I'm scared."

"That just means you get it. I think we're all scared."

A New Plan

We continued to monitor the progress of Little Debbie from the lab. Linda was hanging around more now in order to help wherever she could but was visibly frustrated that she couldn't. Marissa was pinned to the diagnostic information flowing through her screens. We all knew that was her strength and we constantly had hopes she would detect just one more unforeseen pattern that could turn the tables.

Lee and I were working through the details of another possibility together. We discussed the appropriateness of building Big Bertha – a version of Little Debbie on steroids. We kept that in our back pocket but reasoned so long as Little Debbie keeps working, we wouldn't need Big Bertha. Besides, we couldn't be sure that Little Debbie was actually fixing anything. All we could measure was that it was just delaying the inevitable.

"Sean, I've got an idea. We have our doubts about Little Debbie doing what we need. What bothers me most about it is that all we're really doing is changing the TQC from its solid form back to its liquid form. Our tests in the lab showed even the liquid TQC that crossed the threshold can still absorb mass under the right conditions so we have to go farther than that. We need to revert the TQC back to its original state before we ever started messing with it."

"An intriguing thought. I trust you have something in mind?" I responded with sincere interest.

He answered, "I'm thinking we can adapt or extend Little Debbie to be more than an inverse photon transpiler and make it into a fermion phase inverter that alters the angular momentum of electrons causing quantum leaps from outer to inner orbitals. That would necessarily force a breakdown of the TQC nucleus, all the quarks would have to restructure themselves back into to their original base elements. I think it could work. What do you think?"

"Well, quarks have no memory. They have no idea whether they originated from sand or silica or carbon. There would be a certain amount of uncertainty as to which elements it would reduce down to, wouldn't there?" I asked, not because I didn't know the answer but more to prod to see how far he had thought this through.

"I thought of that, but in the big picture what's worse: massive amounts of TQC growing and consuming all of our air; or some large number of metric tons of hydrogen, or oxygen, or carbon, or hell for that matter radioactive uranium? In the former case we all die, and in the latter, we know how to deal with every possible resulting element – even radioactive ones. I know it's a long shot and I'm open to other ideas but I'm feeling like I need to be working on something... anything. What are you thinking about?"

At about that time Marissa entered and said unemotionally, "Sorry to butt in but I've got some more bad news."

That was not what we needed to hear at that time. "Alright, let's hear it. And be gentle please," I said in an ineffective effort to lighten the conversation.

She went on, "I've been watching the rate at which Little Debbie is undoing the cistern and measuring the downward trend of the total mass. What I'm seeing is that Little Debbie is slowing down. The total amount of mass is not decreasing at the same rate it has been."

"Any insight as to why?" I asked.

"It due to one of three things, possibly a combination of all of them. Either Little Debbie is wearing out and just can't go as fast as she used to – which is unlikely; or maybe the workers are getting sloppy and wasting time – again, unlikely because I've been watching them and they are busting butt; or three, the rate of assimilation is increasing such that it is diminishing the work Little Debbie is doing. I believe the last option is most probable.   Furthermore, if this trend continues unaltered, the rate of assimilation will surpass Little Debbie's ability to melt and poor Debbie will never be able to finish the job."

"Well shit. That really sucks. Any more good news Ms. Sunshine?" I asked jokingly.

She replied matter-of-factly, "Hey, don't shoot the messenger."

Turning back to Lee I said, "Ok, that changes our timeline substantially. I do like your fermion phase inverter concept. Not only do I think it has real promise, it's also the only viable option on the table for stopping this. You need to get started on it right now."

Lee replied obediently, "Sure thing. But I'm curious, you are preoccupied with something and that's not like you. You seem kind of distant today." He then innocently added, "Is there something bothering you?"

That was what we needed to break the solemn atmosphere and we all started laughing. "Yeah, I've got a little bit of something on my mind. Is Linda out there? Call her in, there's something I need to talk to everyone about." Linda had been listening just outside the door so she came in immediately.

"I'm here."

"You know we've all agreed to approach this as a worst-case scenario, and that we leave no stone unturned, right?" I began. After the slight silent nods I continued, "I know everyone has been working to figure a way to stop this and I really appreciate the hard work. But we really have to now consider the real worst-case scenario."

Lee hesitantly asked, "What could be worse than not stopping this thing? Isn't that the worst possible scenario? If we fail, we wipe out all of humanity. Do you have something worse than that?"

"No, I don't, but that's not my point. My point is, what if it does turn out that we can't stop this? What do we do then?"

"Does it matter? We're all dead at that point. There can be no other options."

I cautiously proceeded, "Maybe there is another option. If we reach a point where we know we absolutely cannot stop this thing from growing uncontrollably then I think we are obliged to make every effort possible to keep it from ever happening in the first place." I let that sync in for a second or two then added, "Yes, I'm talking about time travel."

Time Travel

Lee and Marissa immediately started laughing and firing off a multitude of mostly rhetorical questions that were all different versions of "My god man, have you lost your mind?" Linda remained silent until the chatter and laughter died down.

She then said simply, "Continue."

Dead silence. The grins disappeared and the jollity ceased. Linda's comment had spoken volumes. With that one single word she told the room to shut up while silently expressing '*I may not be convinced yet but I trust you enough to listen to more*'. I now had everyone's undivided attention so I continued.

"Hear me out, this isn't as crazy as it sounds. I've been thinking about this for years and never thought it would be practical. But here we are. First of all, I'm not talking time travel as you see in all the movies. We're not going to slingshot around the sun and go back in time to save the whales. All we have to do is get a message back to me telling me to help Marissa prove Korkov is right. If we do that, and she does come up with the proof, which we all know she will, then Big Gus never has the problem, Vaduz and Bern go without a hitch and the planet is not doomed.

"So that's the good news. Now let's address the problems and mitigation strategies. First of all, there will be 'future distortion'. Just the act of me reading the message will change our past, but that's not really a bad thing because that is *exactly* what we're trying to do. I'd be hard-pressed to come up with any kind of scenario that would be worse than global planetary annihilation. Nonetheless, in an effort to minimize collateral damage I will be the only one to know. There's lots more we could talk about on this topic like the instant we send the message, you and I cease to be who we are in this timeline, we become who we turn into in the next timeline. Time distortion is immediate, it only gets worse later. All of that is unavoidable and not worth wasting time on now. The new you won't even notice a difference. I'm not sure the word difference is even applicable since there will be nothing to be different from.

"Next, the old me is going to have to believe the message came from me. Look at how you two reacted when I just mentioned time travel. If it isn't convincing enough, I'll just think Lee is pranking me. I've got a plan for this one so let's move on.

"Here's the million dollar question you've been waiting for. How do we do it? That's a tough one and I don't have everything worked out yet. I'm going to need some help from you guys. But the general idea goes something like this.

"Einstein's theory of relativity tells us time dilates and space can warp. For years I pondered this and I'm convinced that time not only dilates, but it also bends. I believe it is possible to bend time to the point it intercepts with itself. It is at that point of intersection that something, in our case an electronic representation of a message, can jump timelines. Now, bending time will require an inordinate amount of energy but here's where it gets sexy. We don't need to bend time over vast expanses of open space like you see in artwork and movies, I'm talking about bending time and 'opening the wormhole' if you want to call it that, at the quantum level. We use quantum tunneling like they do for atomic fusion. All we need to bend is a few picometers, just big enough to let an electronic waveform pass through. At that scale, a little bit of energy goes a long way. And the best part? We already have access to that energy with our fermion particle collider. That's what we use to make lenium."

Lee couldn't hold back any longer. He blurted, "But that energy, while powerful and intense, is only around for infinitesimally small periods of time. It is inconceivable to me that we could hold a 'worm hole' open long enough for an entire message to get through, maybe one or two amplitude cycles but certainly not millions if not billions of cycles."

"Yes, that's true, but we don't have to. Imagine you have a marble that you need to roll down a one-hundred-foot hill. The marble will not roll through grass so you have two ten-foot lengths of pipe that you lay end-to-end. You start the marble at the one end of the first pipe and when it reaches the second length of pipe, you grab the first pipe and rush it down to the other end of the second. The marble eventually arrives and you repeat the process eight more times until you have gone the full one hundred feet. We do the same thing only with the worm hole. We create the first one and start the send of the message then continually build subsequent worm holes at light speed until the message has completely passed.

"Here's another, better way of thinking about it. You have all the seen the magician levitate the beautiful assistant, right? And once he does, he takes a hoop and moves the hoop over and around her floating body to prove there are no strings attached.

We do it just like that only the beautiful assistant is our electronic message and the magician's hoop is a series of transient wormholes the size of the *Planck Length* [9] that keep leapfrogging end-to-end until the wormhole has passed over the message. Same concept, just a bit harder to pull off. The message is travelling light speed in one direction, the wormholes are travelling light speed in the other.

---

[9] The *Planck Length*, named after Max Planck, is the distance a photon would travel in 10^{-43} seconds. 10^{-43} seconds is the *Planck Time* - the smallest division of time that has meaning.

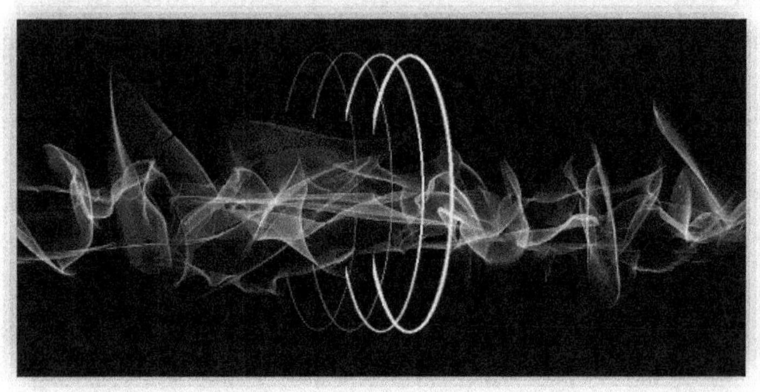

Now was a good time to pause and wait. Lee was thinking. Linda was lost. Marissa was intrigued.

"It could work." I added.

Marissa then volunteered, "One other issue might be that for this message to land where it is supposed to, you are going to have to remember exactly where you were at exactly some precise moment in time from six years ago. Could you tell me where you were, let's say, exactly one year ago today? Specifically, right now?"

I answered, "No, but that doesn't matter. I do know exactly where I was at 13:30 UTC, August 24th, 2060."

"You do?" replied Linda rather astonished.

"I do. 13:30 UTC on that day, which is my birthday by the way, is 6:30 AM PDT. I happen to remember that morning very well, even after six years, and in amazing slow-motion detail." I could see Linda was struggling to remember.

Lee finally reluctantly replied, "I'll do whatever you need from me. I'll get you a pile of strong force energy to use on your moving wormhole hoop thingies, but I have to be honest, I have my doubts."

In response I said, "I know you will, and I know you do. For now, you work on the fermion phase inverter. That is still our single best hope. Now, let's get back to work."

It was obvious he still had doubts because it was still "my wormhole" not "our wormhole". I was confident his buy-in would come later, but it couldn't be that much later. Time, I feared, was running out.

We were leaving the room when I glanced at Linda just as she remembered where she was on my birthday six years ago. I saw her smile.

The Epiphany

Everyone kept working on their appointed tasks. Lee was getting no sleep and I couldn't make him slow down. Periodically he would ask if I needed anything from him. I always responded with "Not now, but the time will come." Marissa was continually monitoring and reevaluating the projected point at which Little Debbie would become useless. It was a race to see if Lee could get his phase inverter done before Little Debbie gave up the ghost. Both were very close. All the while, Marissa kept archiving our work for reasons nobody really understood. She had always done that but now she was doing it with an uncommon zeal and very bewildering timing. Linda speculated it was her way of coping.

I was still struggling with my formula and calculations to bend time around a waveform but I was just missing something. I continued to pour over my time and space calculations all the while hoping I'd never have to use them. It was my fortieth birthday and it was going completely unnoticed for obvious reasons.

I have always been convinced that the cube for intergalactic travel is based on time, distance, and direction in relation to energy and velocity. Relativity tells us that as velocity increases, time dilates. That has been proven through countless experiments going back to the 1970's. But how do I bend time instead of dilating it. Then came the epiphany.

'I've got it! I really think I've got it!' kept echoing through my head. The key is not time, *distance*, and direction, it is time, *space*, and direction. That's what I've been missing. For what I need, direction is linear and space is nearly immeasurable. By refactoring to isolate time as a function of the other values, I can bend time close enough for the quantum tunnel to work. The

risk is all but eliminated and distance becomes irrelevant.

'I really think I've got it.'

Now if only I could test it. I kept trying to think of how I could but it didn't take much reasoning to conclude that any viable test would by definition be subject to future distortion so there was no guarantee that even if it did work, I would even know. It was like the Heisenberg uncertainty principle, the very act of making the attempt would necessarily alter the result. No, the only chance we had was to take the shot, no practicing allowed.

OUT OF OPTIONS

I think everyone was expecting it and dreading it at the same time but finally the time came. Marissa announced that Little Debbie was no longer reducing the total mass, it was just slowing down the growth. She also pointed out that the crew that had been running it quit once they saw they weren't undoing anything anymore. They didn't have the sense to realize quitting only made it speed up more. I asked Lee the status on the phase inverter and he said he still needed time for calibration and optimization. I told him he needed to just "fix forward" and that we needed to get it started. We were just running out of time.

Lee went to the site with Linda to incorporate his work into Big Gus. That part thankfully went flawlessly. He fired it up and we all got a little bit excited by seeing the TQC dissolving away into sand, steam, and other kinds of indescribable rubble I guess you'd call it. We didn't have any resources to test the rubble so we just kept doing what we were doing. After about two hours Lee called in to report that he had completed the calibrations and optimizations on the fly and the phase inverter was running full throttle and better than expected. Everyone was getting hopeful. I told him to come back to the lab to monitor the progress. I wanted us all together.

People were beginning to gather outside the lab. They were scared also and they didn't know how big this problem was growing. Linda had been working with local authorities for security and protection. So far, we were safe but crowds can change in an instant. We had to block that out and stay focused.

While he and Linda were returning, Marissa and I were in the lab where I was preparing the message. It was fully holographic because I knew seeing myself talk would be crucial to convincing me that I was me. Once finished I asked her to drop the framerate from sixty frames per second to one frame per five seconds. I didn't need high quality video but I did need as small of data packet as possible. Marissa informed me there was no such concept of frames per second with holograms because they more resembled structured vector graphics than bitmaps, but she understood the intent and took care of it.

She then asked a strange question, "Sean, is it possible to send a message forward in time as well as backward? I'm curious."

"I'm not even certain it can be sent back in time. But if it can, I suppose going forward is theoretically possible also. If I just toggle the directional constant from -1 to +1 it should do exactly the same thing the other direction. Everything else would be exactly the same, however, same day, time of day, and place, just a different future time of exactly the same increment," I replied, wondering why she wanted to know but not really wanting to pursue it any further at the moment because she seemed satisfied with the answer.

I had reviewed my computations to the point of being dizzy. They would just have to be good enough. Nobody else on the team was capable of checking my work. We were ready as we'd ever be.

When everyone was back together, we got in the room together and went over what we knew was inevitable if Lee's phase inverter didn't work. We acknowledged to each other that once we pushed the button to send the message back in time, if we were all still standing around wondering if it worked then it didn't work. If there was no future distortion it had to have failed. If it did work, we couldn't be standing here wondering because this timeline would no longer exist.

Marissa had one last question to ease her conscience, "Do we even have the right to make this decision for the entire world?"

Linda replied, "Marissa, life has given us only two choices at this juncture, push the button or don't push the button. There is no right or wrong anymore, we will make that decision either through action or inaction. Either way, we're deciding what happens. It sucks, but there it is."

Marissa nodded and it looked like she was slightly relieved.

Last Ditch Effort

"Sean, it's not working."

"Not working? What's not working?"

"The fermion phase inverter. It's not working. The rate of assimilation is now 1.6 times the rate of inversion."

"Can you be more specific please? If it is not working there can be no rate of inversion. So, is it working – yes or no?"

"Sorry. Yes and no. The fermion phase inverter is in fact functioning, in fact, I'm pushing it at an oscillation rate 22 percent above the sustainable threshold. It is doing exactly what it is supposed to do. But that is just not enough, it's not even keeping up. This is not the answer. And we're running out of time."

"How much time do we have?"

"Just a sec... The rate of assimilation is no longer linear; it has gone hyperbolic. Switzerland and most of Austria will be gone in less than six hours. At the current rate of acceleration, no one on this planet will see tomorrow."

"Well shit! We're out of time and out of options. We're going to have to try it, aren't we?

Cheng Le obliged me with a simple sad confirming nod.

I looked around the room and asked, "Everyone ready?"

Marissa said, "No, not yet. Before you send your message would you please toggle your directional constant and send this?"

"What's this?" I asked apprehensively.

She responded simply, "I've got this."

That was good enough for me. One quick change and I sent her message, changed it back and sent mine.

5. THE NEW MIDDLE

> *We cannot solve our problems with the same*
> *thinking we used when we created them.*
> Albert Einstein

THIRTY-FOUR (AGAIN)

"Well shit. I was hoping it wouldn't come to this.
You are really not going to like what you're about to
tell you."

So echoed the familiar and grammatically puzzling voice emanating from my personal iChron.

From a vacation cabin in the Southern Cascades in the Great Northwest, on my 34th birthday, I'm on the deck watching the clouds settle into the valleys between the rolling hilltops. Above the clouds are the snowcapped peaks whose snow line is rising, imperceptible to human observation but rising nonetheless. While I am always struck with awe at the sheer visual splendor of God's work on a grand scale, likewise I will also never stop marveling at the small-scale majesty of the quantum world in the tip of each cloud where the mist seems to magically mutate over time into nothingness. Sheer natural unseen beauty at the other end of the scale.

It's 6:30 AM PDT, August 24 in the year 2060. After a grueling eight and a half years of research, experimentation, writing, review, and rework I'm celebrating the completion and publication of my signature paper *Time, Space and Quanta – Interactions that Challenge Relativity.* I apparently had forgotten to cancel my daily reminder to check my iChron for my running to-do list for the day. Linda wasn't up yet so I thought I'd sneak a peek; she would be disappointed if she found me working while on vacation.

On this particular day I confess I'm slightly bewildered by an entry I ostensibly made dated August 24, 2066, since you would have to go through a lot of trouble to make a typo like that. My fear is that I'm being pranked by Cheng Le, my esteemed associate, who possesses not only a brilliant mind but also a much more playful sense of humor than I. And yet, I can't fathom how he could have defeated the three-factor biometric authentication on the device. Even more than that, I can't deny that is my face and voice, in full holographic form, relaying the foreboding message. I let it continue with skeptical anticipation.

*"I have to keep this short because the longer I talk
and the more I say, the greater the probability of*

altered timelines. So, to keep things succinct I'll get right to the point. You must listen closely.

"You are fucking up! You are on the verge of making the biggest mistake of not just your lifetime but in the history of all humanity.

"Do I have your attention?"

Wow! That sounds really bad.' I sarcastically think to myself now absolutely convinced I'm being pranked.

I am not one prone to use profane expletives – I've always considered their use a speech impediment – and yet, I just heard me use them twice in nearly as many sentences. That's not me. I'm definitely being pranked.

"Now, before you turn me off convinced that you're being pranked, consider the fact that I know things – like the time when you were eleven and you and Robbie would sneak into Mr. Franklin's back yard to peek through the basement bathroom window to watch the nurses who rented a room from him shower. I know for a fact that you've never shared that with anyone. Convinced yet? Well, get convinced, because as I said, I, you, we don't have much time.

"The government grant for your fermion particle collider is about to come through for you. When it does, a cascade of venture capitalists will also come

through providing you with more money than you ever dreamed of to actually build it. You need to build it, but not the way in which it is designed.

Your postulate that fermion ions under gamma ray saturation cause quantum strong forces to bond similar yet different hadrons is fundamentally sound at small to large scale. But, at extremely large scale, there are behavior changes in electromagnetism that introduce entropy at a rate beyond anything the current design can handle. Your colleague, Marissa, whom you haven't met yet, will discover this probability but she will not possess the scientific acumen required and she will need your help to get the science behind it fully vetted.

Do not dismiss her just because she can't prove it. She's got the insight; you've got the knowledge. You need to help her prove it even though it will identify a gap in your thesis. Get over your pride and do it.

"As much as I would like to explain to you what already happened six years from now, I can't take the risk. Just know that I must make every effort to erase my 'footprints' and to minimize the probability of future distortion by returning your timeline to as close to original state as possible. Sending this message has already raised the probability of you altering your future, my history, to a near certainty. Some of that change is desirable and intentional,

everything else is collateral damage that must be minimized. I really wish I could explain in more detail.

"I know you will wonder how I accomplished getting this message to you. Don't worry about it. It's not important. Besides, you will figure it out, after all you are the one who sent it.

"Finally, and not to pile on, but here's some more bad news you have to warm up to preferably sooner than later. Vladimir Korkov's 'Principle of Electron Convergence at Massive Scale' will ultimately be proven right, just not in time for you. The principle is essentially sound it is just his proofs that are flawed. Embrace it now. In fact, you need to help Marissa help him prove it.

"That's all."

'Korkov!' I mentally exclaimed to myself. *'I detest that egotistical self-centered old-timer has-been excuse for a physicist. In his mind, theory trumps fact. When experimental proof cannot be ethically attained, fabricating it with fudged results for the greater good is his mode of operation. He missed his chance due to his own belligerent obstinance...'*

I had much more to say about the man but got pleasantly interrupted by the scent of hot hazelnut coffee wafting onto the deck. I looked up and saw my wife, lover, and confidant Linda carrying two cups and wearing one of my t-shirts. I couldn't tell if she had anything on underneath, but I learned long ago that reality is not a prerequisite to enjoyment, so I just envisioned what I wanted to. It worked. My birthday was beginning to improve.

As she was approaching and taking in the morning sunrise I suddenly panicked. I can't let her see me 'working' so I surreptitiously slipped my iChron under the cushion of my lounger. She came over to me, leaned down and whispered "Happy Birthday" in my ear with that indescribably sensual voice she is able to turn off and on, then gently kissed me on the lips. She held it longer than I was expecting but got no complaints from me.

Sadly, all I'm thinking is *'Cool, I hid it in time.'*

She laid down on the lounger next to me, took a sip of coffee, then turned towards me and said (in her not-so-sensual tone of voice) "You know, it's your birthday and we're on vacation. That's two reasons you do not have a 'to-do' list today."

Busted!

I started to come up with some lame explanation of denial knowing full well I would never use it because I can never lie to Linda. Then I remembered my/his words "erase my footprints". CRAP! That entry is going to disappear. I need to back it up or I will never be able to convince anyone what happened. But how do I pull that off with her right next to me. In a mere instant I seemed to run through multiple scenarios and assessed each one's probability of success then quickly concluded that I'm an idiot for wasting precious time thinking of a plan instead of backing up the entry. So, I pulled out my hidden iChron and before I could respond to Linda's disappointed stare, I noticed that entry had already been replaced with a simple text entry with today's date. It said simply…

"No one but you can know."

I had nothing to share with her now other than a fantastic story about a time traveler, me, from the future, so I made a point of ceremoniously powering the device off in front of her and saying simply "Just wanted to ensure that there was nothing going on to distract me from you today." There was at least a little truth to that, albeit miniscule. I thought I might have heard a cynical, mildly sarcastic, under-the-breath retort of "Yeah, right," but couldn't be sure.

As we lay back absorbing the morning in silence together, I began to question whether or not the now deleted message actually came from the future me. You'd think I'd remember something like that. Proceeding in my physicist probability-oriented mind I questioned myself as to how likely it was that one of those nurses from long ago remembered my nine-year-old face and waited twenty-five years to track me down in a mountain chalet to perform a technically elaborate prank on my birthday. I unscientifically concluded there was zero probability of that. Further scrutiny revealed the logical inference that if there was zero probability of even one other person knowing of the incident then, by definition, the messenger had to be the single person that did indeed possess said knowledge. I had no choice but to accept that I had just been talking to myself. Sometimes Boolean logic can be very liberating even if confusing.

For one fleeting moment I wondered how my day went on my last 34th birthday, but alas, that was a question to remain forever unanswered.

"Let's finish our coffee and go for a hike," I said knowing there was no reason to phrase this as a question. This was a guaranteed-to-be-accepted offer that would serve to help me win back a few of those points I had already lost this morning.

Confirming once again that absolute constants do exist, she replied "That would be wonderful." I was slightly disappointed knowing that she would likely want to put something on other than her hiking boots, but I knew a summer day is long in the Northwest and holding her hand while walking in the woods was a delightful experience – even when fully clothed.

To Tell or Not to Tell

Weeks passed and I was tormented on a daily basis by keeping something of this magnitude from Linda. *'Why hadn't I told me more about what was going on so I could focus where I needed to? I think my consternation is starting to show and Linda is suspecting something. Surely six years from now I didn't mean to exclude Linda,'* I unsuccessfully reasoned. But I couldn't get past the reality that I said, "No one must know," and had I meant anything else I would have used different words.

"I must make every effort to erase my 'footprints' and to minimize the probability of 'future distortion'," I had told myself. No mystery there. Even in this timeframe I would be thinking of minimizing the butterfly effect that must necessarily be caused by messing with time. That thought was anything but satisfying because it only served to confirm that I was now, and continually, participating in changing things in what was my previous future – i.e., future distortion. The whole thing was twisting my brain into knots. I really wished I could ask Linda's advice. Maybe I could if I'm careful.

"Hey hon, can I ask you a philosophical question?" I nonchalantly threw out to test the waters. I'd have to play this one by ear and bail at the first sign of trouble.

"I suppose. What?"

"Do you think there are things that two people in love can't, or maybe shouldn't, share with each other? I mean what if there is an extremely high probability that sharing would be harmful to the other?" I knew it was a vague and risky question almost certain to evoke the reaction I was least prepared to deal with. The one where she asks, *"What are you not telling me?"* In an attempt to deflect that possibility, I thought I'd strike first with "Are there things you don't tell me?"

"Yep." She answered quite matter-of-factly.

"Really?"

"Sure."

"Like what?" I realized I had lost control of the conversation but was now more interested in the answer to this question than anything I'd been thinking.

"Well, for one thing I don't share with you why I prefer Kotex tampons over Tampax," she replied with a quite satisfied voice.

"I was thinking of something more substantial." I pried.

"Oh, you mean like seeing other men?" she asked innocently.

"Not what I had in mind but let's run with it."

"Sure, I hide that stuff too."

"Seriously?" I said trying sound dead pan instead of incredulous.

"Oh sure. Just last week I went out with another man to have drinks," she taunted.

"Who with?" This wasn't fun anymore.

"Bill Bradley, from the English department. He wanted advice on his resume and I told him I'd help," she explained.

"That's not shocking. You could have told me that," I reasoned.

"Yeah, I could have, but didn't. There was no reason to. You would have just looked up from your notepad and said, 'That's nice.' Then I could have said it again ten minutes later and you would have said the same thing again so why bother?" was her response.

She was right, my memory retention filter would have kicked in and asked, *'Remember this or toss it?'* I would have tossed it.

"This isn't helping" I feebly observed.

She then stopped what she was doing and dropped her playful tone, made eye contact with me, and in a sympathetic, disarming, and caring voice said, "Well, I guess this theoretical soulmate of which you speak needs to ask himself – is he protecting me or himself?" Her use of the word "me" was clearly her way of putting all the pretense aside.

Then, with a particularly satirical attempt at talking to me in a language I could understand she continued, "Perhaps the best thing to do would be to identify the probabilities of the alternatives weighted against the probabilistic harm of each alternate outcome to determine the best and/or least destructive course of action," which was followed by a short pause. "Or you could just tell me what the hell is going on and I'll let you know if you should have told me or not," she closed with while heading to the kitchen so as to not put any more pressure on me.

I really liked that last option but wasn't ready to pull the trigger just yet.

THE BIG REVEAL

I was at home in the living room with my notepad and pencil. Linda wasn't home yet from her *Helping Heroes Help Themselves* event. Normally I'd be in my 'ready room' working on something related to work but today I was just pondering the ominous message I had gotten from my future self and wishing I could talk all this over with Linda. In doing so I kept doodling on my notepad certain phrases:

"Help Marissa help Korkov";
"changes in electromagnetism that introduce entropy";
"large scale";
"Korkov is proven right";
"Don't dismiss Marissa".

I just kept thinking to myself, over and over, like in some kind of time loop, *'What did I mean about large scale and introducing entropy? And who is this Marissa I don't know and have never met. What if my future has already been changed and I never meet this Marissa?'* I know I was more than a little disappointed that Korkov was still in my present timeline.

I guess it was around 6:15 PM when Linda got home. As she entered, I heard her shout the traditional "Honey, I'm home." Once in the door she saw I was in the living room and she said to me, "Come here, there's someone I'd like you to meet." So, I stood up and began walking toward the door. There was something just a little bit mischievous about their interactions. I was pretty sure I'd find out what soon enough.

"Sean, meet Marissa…" she got out after which I did a double take and accidently hit my shin on the coffee table. While I stumbled around suppressing the expletives that wanted to jump out of my mouth, she managed to complete her sentence, "and Marissa, this is Sean."

193

"Hi Marissa, pleased to meet you," I replied fairly certain that I didn't include "in more ways than one" although that would have been wholly applicable. My eyes fixated on Marissa's face. *'This is her! She is in my timeline after all. Maybe now I find out what all this means. Man, this is creepy!'* Once I felt Linda's icy stare, I realized they were both getting uncomfortable due to my transfixion on Marissa's face.

"As I was saying," she continued, "Marissa was an incredible help today. She took care of all computer and networking issues for us. Now all the office computers can talk to each other."

"Sounds like you were needed today," was all I could manage.

"Thank you, Mr. Blake. Linda exaggerates a little, it was a team effort and it was educational and fun."

"Please, call me Sean. And come into the living room and have a seat. You can tell me how you two met. Would anyone like a drink?"

"No thanks," said Linda.

"No thanks, but don't let that stop you," was Marissa's response.

"Oh, it won't. I'm definitely having a drink," I muttered to myself that was hopefully inaudible to them.

Once everyone was seated Linda and Marissa summarized their day and explained how Marissa got out of class to help. After that, Linda started to tout the laurels of Marissa's acumen for quantum physics and quantum computing. Linda looked surprised that I wasn't surprised, it was almost a look of disappointment.

"So, what aspects of quantum physics are you studying? What floats your boat so to speak?" I asked.

Marissa recognized the setup was complete. It was time to execute the prank they had planned and to lay it on and lay it on heavy. Linda was starting to smile but with some reservation.

"I guess in addition to all the normal mainstream stuff, right now I'm completely taken up by the fascinating work a guy named Vladimir Korkov is doing on electron convergence. Everything I've read by him I find absolutely mind blowing. That man has forgotten more than I could ever hope to know about nuclear cohesion," she started with, then just kept going on and on about how big and great Korkov was. I didn't hear much of it because my brain was looping through all the phrases I had been doodling earlier, only now I was thinking them much louder, especially the '*Korkov is right*' which was second only to '*do not dismiss Marissa.*'

I squeezed out a reply, "Yes, I find a lot of his ideas titillating. What part of his work most intrigues you?

For example, do you think that the *Korkov Constant* actually exists?"

Marissa exhibited a small amount of panic as she exchanged a quick glance with a befuddled Linda then proceeded to explain that she agreed with his views of electromagnetism introducing entropy and that she felt he would ultimately be proven right. I mentioned that I also felt those ideas were quite plausible just unproven.

That was it. Linda made up some excuse about a previous engagement she had forgotten about and politely and apologetically asked Marissa to leave, which Marissa did. Linda then came back into the living room and stood right in front of me.

"Ok. What was THAT!" she demanded.

"What was what?" I knew what she meant but wasn't sure if this was something I'd be able to duck.

"What you ask? Everything what! First there was that google-eyed stare you gave Marissa right in front of me, that embarrassed the crap out of both her AND me, we'll come back to this one later, but the part about Korkov being titillating?" she said while doing air-quotes with two fingers on each hand. "Well, 'Lucy, you've got some splaining to do,'" she said in a horrible imitation of Ricky Ricardo, followed by, "I want an answer and I want it now. And think very carefully before you say a word."

It was apparent I wasn't going to duck this one. I handed her my notepad and said, "Here, take a look at this." In a very deadpan tone of voice.

She paged forward then back again. After making eye contact with me she said, "H-o-l-y s-h-i-t!"

"Want to hear the rest of the story?"

"I'm not sure. Do I?"

"I don't think there's a choice anymore."

I proceeded to tell her the whole story, the message, what it contained, how it disappeared and was replaced by the text-only message. Everything I knew to tell her, I told her.

She then asked, "So, is this what you wanted to talk to me about last week but didn't? All that soulmate stuff and keeping secrets to protect your partner?"

"Yep. And you said maybe I should just tell you and you'd let me know if it was the right thing to do or not, remember? Well, was it? Was it the right thing to do?"

"Too soon to call. Ask me again in six years," she said before adding, "You do realize we can't tell Marissa or Lee, right? This has to stay between you and me."

"No question about that," I confirmed.

MARISSA MEETS LEE

Work was continuing and Lee was making great progress. It was clear to Linda and me that we had no choice but to recruit Marissa for the team. I was pleased when Linda told me she had been thinking Marissa would be a good fit even before she knew of the message. We strategized as to how to pull it off and Linda offered to fall on the proverbial sword so as to make me not look so stupid. She felt it was more important for Marissa to respect me than her.

One day soon after I met Marissa, Linda invited her down to the lab. Marissa was more than willing, she was excited. Once she was there, we introduced her to Lee and showed her around. At one point she heard Lee griping about some kind of integration problem he was having. Marissa overheard him and went over to take a look. I couldn't hear exactly what they were talking about but it had something to do with subnet masks and protocols. Whatever it was, it was a stroke of good luck because it seemed to fix whatever problem Lee had been having.

"Where did you find this woman?" was Lee's query to Linda and me. "I think I like her."

"Good to know. I like her too." I replied so that Marissa could hear.

And with that, Linda took Marissa just out of earshot of both of us to talk her into joining. I couldn't hear a thing but as I watched I could just tell how Linda was proceeding through all the talking points we had discussed earlier. First, she brings up the night we met in order to explain things and clear the air. She confesses that I had been bothered by a secret I hadn't shared with her. She wouldn't share what the secret was but she did offer that when Marissa mentioned Korkov's name, I became concerned that the secret was out. Before she was done, she would explain that I had had some kind of religious experience and felt convicted that I had let my ego keep me from viewing Korkov's work objectively and that now I would probably be a good person to talk to about the subject. All of that was true on some level and only slightly distorted. It was effective though because Linda was able to bring Marissa on board. She would later take care of formally finalizing the agreement with an NDA and all the other legal paperwork Lee had to do.

SEAN.V1 AND SEAN.V2

One night Linda and I were home, cuddled up under a blanket on the couch watching a movie called *Frequency*. We had seen it numerous times before but thought it appropriate because it was about time travel. Well, not so much time travel as much as communicating across time. I won't spoil it for you, but as with all sci-fi time travel stories there is always one insurmountable flaw in the story line. It is always different depending on the story but there always is one. In this one, one character is allowed to remember all of his timelines while the rest of the world has only one perspective. They could have corrected that but then the movie would have been really boring because nobody would know timelines were changing.

Anyway, as we watched we talked about our situation and we speculated on what had happened in our previous future vs. what was happening now. The problem was it got confusing talking about me because there was the first Sean that *sent* the message, and the second Sean that *received* the message. We agreed to name them Sean.V1 and Sean.V2 respectively, then quickly shortened them to simply V1 and V2.

On this particular night I was feeling rather existential and I posed a paradoxical question to Linda about whether or not Sean.V1 ever existed, does exist, or ever will exist.

"It is not possible that he never existed because if he never existed then Sean.V2 could not exist because V2 is dependent on V1 sending the message. Therefore, since we know V2 does in fact exist..." I postulated before I was interrupted.

"Objection. That's a fact not in evidence," she playfully injected.

I replied, "Je pense, donc je suis."

"Huh?"

"French not your bag? How about the language of lawyers then? *'Cogito ergo sum'*".

"And in English?" she persisted.

"I think, therefore I am" I replied with conviction.

"Overruled." She conceded with a chuckle.

I continued, "Since we've established that V2 does exist, it can only be reasoned V1 did at one time exist. It also follows logically that since V1 will send a message backward in some number of years from now, he must exist in the future. Furthermore, if he exists in the future and is older than me, then he must be born already and has not yet experienced death. That means he must, by logical inference, exist in the present. And by the way, that same logic is equally applicable to the past," I concluded.

No reaction from Linda, so I continued.

"So even though every form of logical reasoning tells us Sean.V1 exists in the past, present and future, we observe that he is, in fact, nowhere to be found. There is no verifiable proof of his existence or that he ever existed other than one easily faked text-only entry on a device."

Then for the kick butt conclusion, "Therefore we have proven that time, in addition to dilating, must also bend and in fact even intersect with itself. Do you not concur?" It was a stretch conclusion but someday I intended to prove it. But right now, I had other things to ponder.

"A noble dissertation for sure," Linda said, playing into my fantasy. "And since you seem bent pursuing the esoteric, have you considered the legal implications?

'Uh oh,' I thought. *'When she talks in her lawyer voice these conversations rarely end well for me.'* "Like what?" I questioned.

"Well, like I married Sean.V1 and now since you have proven that he never died and I certainly have never been divorced, Sean.V2 must be having an affair with a married woman. And that's grounds for divorce."

"But then that means that you are cheating on your husband with me," I argued back.

"Think you can prove that?"

"If you can prove your point, I can prove mine," was my defiant reply.

"Are you sure of that? I'll be representing myself so I'm quite confident I'll have a better lawyer than you."

"Touché. Mea culpa." It turned out just like I expected it would.

"I have more. Want to hear them?"

"Nah. That's ok."

"You're just not the same man you used to be," she said with a giggle.

"Ok, that's enough."

"You're the only person I know who talks to themself in the third person."

"Stop it! You're killing me."

We finished watching the movie before I got serious again. "But seriously, I'm going crazy second guessing every move I make. Am I making the same bad decisions that Sean.V1 made? How can I know? Or am I fixing the problems that V1 implored me to fix?"

After some contemplation Linda replied, "Well, personally, I don't give a shit. All my money is riding on V2 and V1 can go suck eggs. In fact, I make this vow to you that from this day forward I will never again sleep with Sean.V1. And you Sean.V2, should come to bed with me now."

And with that, the day was officially done.

6. ANOTHER CHANCE

> *You never fail until you stop trying.*
> Albert Einstein

A NEW ELEMENT

Lee was making continued progress with the development of the *molecular electron exciter* which we referred to as MEE. He was very close to the fabrication of the 119th element of the periodic table which would have the largest atomic weight of any element known to man and which would have an unprecedented number of valence electrons in multiple suborbitals of the eighth shell.

We had received a small government grant that enabled us to purchase some much needed equipment which excited Marissa greatly – a Q-Tron Hyper 4000 quantum computer and an industrial sized 3-D printer. She was busy writing the programs for generating small farm tools out of TQC on the 3-D printer. Much to her dismay I would pull her off of what she was working on to direct her toward thinking about the *Korkov Constant*. I was certain that was critical for us to avoid our mistakes of the past, or rather, our future.

One Tuesday morning I spoke with Marissa, "Marissa, have you had a chance to run any more projections on the cohesion factors of large mass?"

"Not yet. I thought it was more important to get the programming for done for a few products since Lee appears to be right on the brink of finalizing the fermion particle collider. We're planning on sharing our progress with Linda on Thursday you know. Was that not right?" she innocently asked.

I responded gently, "No, that's fine, we need that too. What all do you have done that you can produce right now?"

"I can do a shovel blade and rake head right now and I'm working on a comb and some miscellaneous weeding tools right now. I'm pretty close to having them done also," she replied.

"Well, what you already have will be fine for Thursday, but go ahead and finish what you can for the rest of today but tomorrow, done or not, I want you to focus on electromagnetic entropy we expect to get introduced when we hit the large mass nucleus of lenium. I've got some calculations that account for the mass and density of the atomic weight but I'm still missing something. Between the two of us I think we can get this figured out. Does that work for you?"

"Sure thing chief. You're the boss."

It was only about two hours later that Lee chimed up triumphantly, "Finally, I think I've got it stabilized," he shouted to the room. "Sean, come take a look."

Marissa and I walked over to his part of the lab and he tossed a marble sized ball of a clay-like substance in my direction. I caught it and asked, "Is this what I think it might be?"

"Trilenium Quadra Chloride!" he declared. "If that's what you were thinking, then it is what you think it might be. I finally figured out the proper way to initiate the bonding once the fermion particle collider produced the lenium but before it had a chance to decay. The trick was removing some of my debugging code which was slowing the process down just enough to cause trouble. It's just like Heisenberg said, my attempts to observe the process altered the results. Now I just need to remove the other debug steps and it should work faster and even more efficiently. The next and final step is the TQC transducer to harden it. I figure there's no reason to not use some of Marissa's shaping and carving up of the TQC before hardening. I'm not expecting any issues there at all given our early experiments. And we've already learned that demos of unusable pencils don't really sell the message."

"Spectacular! Nice work you two," I congratulated. "Have you any idea how far this can scale in mass and density before the electromagnetic nucleic cohesion is affected?"

"Sheesh, Sean, this is just the first baby steps. We've got time and we'll get there. But today, I'm going to take a celebratory lap around the track so to speak."

"You're right of course. I'm just a little antsy that we're missing something fundamental that could be devastating if we don't handle it properly. But you're right. Today is a good day. Again, nice work."

Thursday rolled around faster than I could have imagined. Lee had cleaned up the collider and Marissa had 'printed' the shovel blade and rake head she had done on Tuesday. Linda came into the room and we shared the progress with her. She had a few questions about recyclability and threats by terrorists but nothing substantial that wasn't easily addressed. We were all very satisfied with the results so far but Linda and I weren't really ready to celebrate too much. We both knew there was something about large scale that was looming over our heads. And that needed to be addressed completely before we could fully celebrate. But just what was the problem to be solved? All we knew was it was related to Korkov's work and Marissa was the key.

Once we had shown Linda all there was to show we remained in the room to discuss the possible problems we might observe at large scale. We talked about Korkov's work and speculated on what mistakes he might be making and/or what limitations he had that was preventing him proving his theory. My questions were mostly directed at Marissa for obvious reasons even though both Marissa and Lee found that strange.

After one of my questions Marissa volunteered, "One limitation that we know Korkov has that we now don't, is that all of his work is limited to the first 118 elements. We now have an element that is heavier than all of them at the molecular level and there's a density that we can control. I'm nearly positive that we could validate the *Korkov Constant* if we just knew more about his work. I'm guessing the same is true of him if he had access to lenium and TQC."

"Sean and I believe that this gap in understanding is a potential deal-breaker for the project if left unsolved," Linda stated. "For that reason, I've setup a meeting with Korkov next week in Prague. Marissa, do you like to travel?"

"Europe? Are you kidding? Count me in. Are you saying I will get to meet with Korkov personally?" she replied gleefully.

"That's the plan," Linda confirmed.

Korkov Meets Marissa

Linda and I were on our way to pick up Marissa for our trip to Prague. Lee was staying back to work on getting fermion particle collider, the molecular electron exciter and the TQC transducer all integrated into one single piece of hardware we would call *Big Gus*. He was focused initially on a form factor that resembled a military flame thrower – a backpack and a handheld nozzle for the TQC placement. He figured scaling larger would be simple once the details were worked out.

We flew business class on a Boeing 747 for the fourteen-hour flight because we knew that way we would have accommodations for the three of us to meet and plan strategy and discuss ground rules. It was a little tricky because we couldn't be completely up front with Marissa about our motivations, all we could do was discuss what we could and couldn't share and frankly, there wasn't much we weren't ready to lay on the table. Linda laid out the ground rules.

"The main thing we need to be clear about is that we have to make this relationship work, pretty much at any cost. Now Korkov has an ego bigger than this plane, we can leverage that if we handle it properly. Marissa, we're going to do a little role playing. You are going to play the enamored underling who has always been an admirer. Just keep assuring him how much confidence you have in his intellect and keep asking all those questions you have regarding mass vs. density. I really believe he will open up to you far more than he will with Sean. There's too much history between him and Sean to overcome in a single meeting. We'd like to share as little as possible about our work all the while extracting as much as we can about his, but I'm suspecting we're going to have to give up much more information than we would like. If in doubt at any time, just look at me. I'll find a way to let you know."

Marissa asked, "Are we going to show him samples of the TQC, both solid and liquid forms?"

Sean took over, "That will be unavoidable. We will however deflect questions regarding the calculations and processes of the proton cannon and the TQC transducer. We want him to reflect on the current reality of a compound whose mass exceeds all others while its density is a fraction of the mean density of others. You need to keep prodding him for the experiments that didn't work for him because those are where the real learnings are to be found."

"Got it," she affirmed.

We eventually completed our planning and Marissa went to her seat for some private time to think about what she would be asking. Linda and I were alone and free to talk.

"Are you sure we're doing the right thing by dealing with the devil so to speak?" I asked her.

"We've got to do what we've got to do. You know the consequences of failure so that actually makes answering the question easy," she pointed out.

I argued, "You know that he will take whatever knowledge we give him, claim it as his own, acknowledge no one, and rush to get published so as to be the first. He'll be able to monetize all of our work for his own benefit and we'll be left watching him gloat."

"You're right, he'll probably try but you're forgetting one thing."

"That being?" I quizzed.

She responded with finality, "I've got this."

We arrived in Prague on-time and our escort to the hotel was waiting for us. We got checked in and met in the dining room for dinner and light conversation before retiring. There was no talk about work. In the morning we were taken to Korkov's residence where he did most of his book work and writing. This would be a venue more conducive to our conversation than a lab. We were greeted at the door by a pleasant middle-aged woman who took us through the house to Dr. Korkov's office then bid us adieu.

"Ah, Dr. Sean Blake. We finally meet face-to-face. Welcome to Prague."

"Yes, it has been a long time coming Dr. Korkov, and I am pleased and honored that you have made the time to make this meeting possible," I cordially replied. I then thought I'd address the elephant in the living room right off the bat. "We are both aware of the harsh criticism I have had for your work over the years and I'm welcoming today as one in which I get to correct some of the mistakes of my past if you would allow me to."

"Well, that would be most welcome," he replied with a stunned look.

I continued, "In recent months I must confess I've been enlightened by the thinking and viewpoints of my highly valued colleague who has followed your work for years.   Dr. Korkov, please meet Marissa Faraday. Marissa, Dr. Vladimir Korkov."

"Ms. Faraday, I'm very pleased to meet you."

"Please, call me Marissa."

"Very well, Marissa," he cordially replied before turning to Linda. "And you must be the lovely Dr. Linda Blake. My personal assistant, Marcella, seems to be quite fond of you. I've been instructed to be very hospitable," he added with a smile.

Linda responded in kind and complemented Marcella. With the introductions out of the way we sat at a table and began the conversations.

Korkov opened with, "Dr. Blake, you have travelled a long way, so please tell me, what can I help you with?"

"You can call me Sean."

He dismissed me with "I would prefer to address you by your well-deserved title Dr. Blake."

"As you wish," I replied, "As for your question, we are doing some work with quantum molecular bonding that we feel, I feel, could benefit from your work. It may in fact depend on your work. I think your concepts have great potential and we would like very much to help you prove your theory. Having a defined and validated *Korkov Constant* could help us avoid issues we anticipate we will run into downstream if we don't deal with it up front."

"Exactly what kind of work are you doing with quantum molecular bonding that would benefit from knowing the existence of the *Korkov Constant*?" was the counterpoint.

And with that the conversation began. We explained in as few words as possible the general concept of QC while constantly trying to pull information from him. Linda eventually took over the conversation to address the concerns related to the information sharing and suggest a well thought out arrangement whereby we would share everything we had with him with the understanding that we have a "no compete" agreement stating that he could not ever enter any business, charity or other activity that would use QC concepts. In return, he would maintain complete ownership of the scientific aspects of and full authorship of all work among the scientific community.

Once there was an agreement of intent the conversation went into the science. Marissa kept pressing him to consider the relationship between mass and density. She postulated for his scrutiny that strong forces of nuclear cohesion do in fact tend to alternate amplitudes under situations of large scale and therefore shift to weak forces. The exchange was friendly and helpful. This went on for hours until eventually we all agreed that we could all mutually benefit from sharing data. And with that Linda, Marissa, and I took our leave and returned to the hotel. After a good night's sleep, we returned back home.

All the while, I kept questioning whether I was doing enough and whether I was solving the right problem. How could I ever know?

LIFE IS GRANDER

All the work was paying off and QC was running full bore on small to intermediate runs. Many new products were hitting the shelves and demand for more and better products was increasing. Linda and I were hesitant to take on the larger runs and projects. We didn't know where the threshold was. The larger that the runs got, the more trepid we got about continuing. *The*

Consortium was getting irritated that we were throttling production and rollout beyond anything visible. There were no overwhelming social issues, demand was high, public acceptance had been proven long ago. Linda and I were the only ones who knew why we were doing what we were doing. And we were starting to doubt ourselves also.

Marissa had continued to share information back and forth with Korkov. It was apparent he preferred working with her over me because he felt I was still a threat and he could easily dominate a woman. He was wrong on both accounts.

One afternoon Marissa approached me to look over the math for a particular algorithm she had for running simulations of molecular binding with different variations of TQC isotopes. I offered a few suggestions that would allow her to adapt it more easily to variations. She then set up a series of simulations with Q-Tron, each time the simulation would be altered with a single incremental change to the density/mass ratio and predict where the amplitude fluctuation began. Her tests generated massive amounts of data which she spent countless hours and days correlating and analyzing. Eventually, her work paid off. She identified the controlling threshold whereby regardless of how total nuclear mass was increased or decreased, the application of the constant to electron excitation energy forced the resultant waveforms to superposition themselves maintaining a flatline trajectory over time.

She had proved the *Korkov Constant* was real.

We ran batteries of other simulations without leveraging the newly found constant and each time we predicted with mathematical certainty the results. She had graphics displays tracking the critical factors of mass, density, the threshold, and electromagnetic waveforms. In all cases with the constant used, the waveforms aligned perfectly and destructive interference forced the flatline delta. Without the constant, the waveforms aligned right up to the threshold point then began to diverge just like clockwork. With some simple math we were able to prove that the constant would hold for any amount of density vs mass ratio.

Lee took a look and after asking a few questions, first of Marissa, then of me, he offered to incorporate the constant into Big Gus's molecular electron exciter. He wasn't nearly as excited as Marissa because as he put it, "It won't change anything we're doing." He was right, we had never attempted any run that would come close to approaching the threshold. Marissa, on the other hand was quite excited that she beat Korkov to the punch on his own work. She couldn't wait to fill him in.

What bothered me was that even with it incorporated and knowing that Big Gus would perform differently with it than without it, it did little to appease my worries because I didn't really know what I needed to fix. I had done what my future self had asked me to do, I helped Marissa prove Korkov right, but that was it. Even knowing how the waveforms deviated amplitude beyond the threshold, we still didn't know how that would manifest without actually trying it. This condition had never existed in nature before and therefore it was impossible to predict behavior. How could that deviation possibly be responsible for total planetary annihilation? I didn't know, and probably never would.

7. THE BEGINNING OF FOREVER

> *Try not to become a man of success but rather*
> *try to become a man of value.*
> Albert Einstein

LIFE GOES ON

From this point forward things progressed almost perfectly to plan. Everything Linda had predicted and planned for was happening. People were prospering in places that had never seen prosperity. It took less money to live because so many things were cheap to acquire. Taxes were dropping, charitable giving was catching on, space exploration was exploding, the arts were expanding, nearly every level of life was benefiting either directly or indirectly from the benefits of *Quantum Construction Enterprises.*

Years went by and projects got bigger and bigger and more successful each time. The first big project was a bridge in Vaduz, Austria, which was followed by a water reclamation project in Bern, then on to Japan where TQC was earthquake proofing all the business and home structures.   Roads all over the world were being resurfaced and in fact we now had completed so many projects that we were creating new businesses for using the fermion phase inverter to 'melt' the solid TQC and reclaim the liquid form to be reused elsewhere.

Vladimir Korkov has become a world-renowned physicist and global humanitarian for his work in uncovering and proving the *Korkov Constant*. Marissa received a bouquet of roses from him in thanks for her contributions but that was as far as it went. Her name was never mentioned and he did not acknowledge any of the data that was handed to him by *Quantum Construction Enterprises*. He did, however, inform the world that our process was just one beneficiary of his work and without his work all this prosperity could not exist. I don't know. Maybe he was right. Maybe not.

Korkov had also taken the concepts we shared with him regarding energy conservation of strong force and found a way to manipulate it for his new entertainment company called *Be There Yesterday*™ which is a commercial 'airline' which he promoted as *The first choice for interstellar travel*™. Of course, in true Korkov style none of that was true but it sure sounded good and looked great in all the ads. There were no interstellar destinations because who would want to visit a black hole or imploding red dwarf. And I laughed at the name because even though you traveled very fast and experienced massive time dilation, no matter where you went you still didn't get there yesterday, it was always still just later that same day – just not as late as it might have been.

It didn't matter, we were living quite comfortably. I never worried about budgeting for some new toy, I just asked Linda if we could and she always responded "Sure, we can do that." I asked her once about that over wine and dinner.

"Hey hon, I've got a question for you. We struck a deal with *The Consortium* for compensation of ten million dollars, right? It seems to me I've been spending a lot of that on lab equipment and experimental toys. Are you really sure we're doing OK financially?"

"There are things I don't bother to tell you. You like it that way, you know," she replied distantly.

"Yeah, usually, but I'm curious now. Did you just invest that money wisely and that's why we're so comfortable?"

"Yes and No," she replied wryly with a smile. "Yes, I invested our ten million dollars wisely but no, that's not why we're so comfortable. Let me fill you in on some of the legal aspects of our little agreement with Korkov you are not aware of. In addition to the 'no compete' clause that he agreed to, I added some additional stuff just because. You know we never placed any restrictions on how he could leverage any information he gained from us so long as it didn't compete or conflict with *The Consortium*, right? So, I put in a clause that should any of that information be used in any commercial undertaking that would go public, we were entitled to stock options at ten percent of the ground floor public offering. So now, *Be There Yesterday* is a multibillion-dollar company and what that means to us is that little clause in that one paragraph on page fourteen of the contract is now worth somewhere around $474 million, I haven't checked the exact amount lately."

"That is so cool! I mean, the money is cool and all but just making Korkov give up that much to us is quite satisfying," I exclaimed.

She ended with, "I thought you'd like it."

We went on with dinner in silence, mostly. Whenever I had time to reflect the same questions always kept coming back to me. I couldn't help but ask her just one more time.

"Do you think we did what was necessary? I still worry about it. There's so many 'what if' scenarios that run through my mind because we just don't know how far in the future the problem began."

With a polite and equally firm voice she replied, "I refuse to engage in this discussion anymore. Quit torturing yourself. If we didn't do enough and things go south just figure out what you did the first time and do it again. But please, this time provide enough information when you talk to yourself so that you can be satisfied with the solution when you ultimately save the world again."

She was right. I had to work on that.

SEAN TURNS 46

From a vacation cabin in the Southern Cascades in the Great Northwest, on my 46th birthday, I'm on the deck watching the clouds settle into the valleys between the rolling hilltops. It's become a birthday tradition over time, only now we own the chalet.

It's 6:30 AM PDT, August 24. The last fifteen years had been a whirlwind of excitement. We were living quite comfortably now and this morning as our habit in the summer we were taking in the sunrise from our mountain resort. I could soon smell that fragrance of hazelnut coffee wafting across the deck. I looked up and there was Linda in her terry cloth robe carrying two cups of the java. She approached me and set one cup down next to me while giving me a quick kiss and whispering "Happy Birthday dear" in my ear.

"Have you checked your to-do list yet today?" she asked casually as she took her place next to me. There was a time long ago when doing that would have been considered an act of treason but these days it had become a mandatory part of life.

"Nope, not yet. I'll take a look, but I'm positive I cleared my schedule yesterday." And with that I took a look. I was totally surprised to find an entry. It was a simple entry with an attachment. The entry said simply "Read this.   Marissa" and the attachment was titled *Quarks of Nature.* I opened the attachment and started looking around through it, paging down and up and back again.

Linda became curious about the activity and asked, "What is it? What are you looking at?"

I replied, "Come take a look at this. It looks like some sort of science fiction story that apparently Marissa wrote, only it isn't very polished for being a story. But it sure has a lot of our science included. Come here, you have to see this."

Linda came over and we read everything together. We got to the end of a fantastic story about global planetary annihilation and time travel. The thing was, all the characters were real. They were us, all of us. It ended with the guy named Sean sending a message to himself six years back in time while the world was collapsing. The weird part was that the message he sent was verbatim the *exact same* message I had received some twelve years prior. It even had the story of me and Robbie. He sent the message, then the story just abruptly ended. What a sucky ending.

"Did you ever tell Marissa about the message? We agreed that we wouldn't tell anyone," I asked being slightly perturbed but mostly bewildered.

"I never said a word," she confirmed.

"Well then, how could she even..." I started to speculate. Then WHAM! It hit me.

"Linda, this isn't a science *fiction* story, it is science *fact*. Think about it. If you didn't tell anybody, and I only told you, then *nobody* but us knew about the message except the people who sent it."

"But you sent it, not Marissa."

"I sent it, but like she pointed out in the story, Marissa edited the hologram framerate of the message, so she knew. Not our Marissa, Marissa.V1 if you follow me."

We sat in stunned silence. The implications were astounding. Both of us individually kept assembling the timelines as we realized the whole story of how we got where we are today. All of my nagging, haunting, self-torturing questions had been put to rest.

I marveled at the insight she had to omit critical parts of formulas and write it in such a way that if it fell into the wrong hands, it would be quickly dismissed as just a bad novel. It was no such thing.

"She always did like recording things for posterity. What's ironic is that our Marissa, Marissa.V2, has no idea she did this," Linda added reflectively.

"Should we tell her? Her and Lee?" I asked fully knowing the answer.

"Oh, hell yeah! What possible harm could there be?"

The End

About the Author

I was born in 1955 in Wichita, Kansas to second generation German immigrants from Russia. I grew up in a house filled with love and six kids. I think I got to seventh grade before I learned that not everybody spent their summers visiting aunts and uncles in western Kansas, milking cows, riding horses, and slopping pigs.

I grew to become a campfire guitar player, frustrated rock star, and occasional singer-songwriter. In 1980 I got on my motorcycle and spent three months travelling the United States – that was the summer that Mount Saint Helens erupted. Unable to secure any kind of employment in the Great Northwest and I returned to Kansas to "get marketable"

It was ten years between high school graduation and college graduation where I earned a B.S. in Computer Science with minors in Math and Musicology. Shortly thereafter I had the added bonus of meeting Rhonda who became my wife and the mother of my four magnificent children.

After twenty-five years of employment at Microsoft, most recently in the *A.I. and Machine Learning* group where I built high scale globally connected cloud-based services, I retired.

Now, with time on my hands and a newfound interest in quantum mechanics, I wrote a novel about time travel. No one is more surprised than I.